# Bernie Doing Better

## The MELLIFLUOUS sequel to "Little Boy Bruised"

## Bernard Mendoza

Grosvenor House
Publishing Limited

The right of Bernard Mendoza to be identified as the author of this
work has been asserted in accordance with Section 78
of the Copyright, Designs and Patents Act 1988

The book cover is copyright to Bernard Mendoza
Book cover design by Brian Jones

This book is published by
Grosvenor House Publishing Ltd
Link House
140 The Broadway, Tolworth, Surrey, KT6 7HT.
www.grosvenorhousepublishing.co.uk

This book is a work of fiction based on a true story and real events. Some
names and characteristics have been changed, some events and timelines have
been compressed and some dialogue has been recreated.

Warning: Contains explicit language of a sexual nature

A CIP record for this book
is available from the British Library

ISBN 978-1-83975-938-3

For Paula

# *INTERMISSION*

"Intermission? Who starts anything with an intermission?" says Mel, bumping me shoulder-to-shoulder as she sees the word appear.

"I'm just trying something out." I continue typing. "Some families," I begin again, "will argue over anything. Others are peace and tranquillity personified and value those qualities above all else..."

"Sounds like... Tolstoy," Mel suggests – diffidently, you might say. Even hesitantly.

"It's supposed to. When did you do Tolstoy?"

"Last year we were at school. I quite enjoyed it. We didn't get all the way through...."

"Not surprised. But what you did...you enjoyed?"

"Mmm. It was okay."

"I'm sure Tolstoy was glad to hear that."

"Stupid," she corrects me, bumping me on the shoulder again. "He's dead!"

"I know that. If you remember the quote, he was talking..."

"Writing!"

"..Writing about happy and unhappy families. Right at the very beginning."

"And what's brought this on?" She looks me straight in the eye.

"I've been thinking about us getting married and, especially about the reception. Do you think we could disappear by ourselves one weekend and just do it?"

"They'd..." she was trying to get some words out. "They'd....they'd..."

"..get over it," I finished for her.

# CHAPTER 1

MEL WAS GOOD FOR ME. As the days, the weeks, went by, we were discovering happiness overlaid on happiness. We fitted together, we said, like parts of a Rolex – the kind you could only ever dream of owning, not that we'd ever thought of such a thing.

More important, both our families had sued for peace and left us to get on with our lives.

Mel was astonishing and I loved her to bits. Not only was she mature beyond her years; she was so naturally composed and sensible. A good thing one of us was, did I hear you say?

She kept me on the rails when I got daft ideas. Both of us cooked and cleaned.

We enjoyed love-making enormously.

And slept like cats.

We'd decided we'd get married when Mel reached 21. In the meantime, we saw no point in stirring up the two sleeping dogs that were our families and, in the process, create a more permanent rift.

More to the point, we weren't costing them any money - much to my father's delight, no doubt. They also knew we were enjoying life far better than they could ever have imagined, let alone have predicted. We'd proved our point, growing up so much faster than ever they had.

Since we'd been together, we'd acquired a growing circle of similar-minded friends, comfortable in themselves and with each other. (Who says the Danes invented Hygge?) They included lovely Aggi. She and Mel had become bosom pals, gossiping and giggling. It made me feel good - though I did sometimes wonder who the giggles were intended for.

I'd stopped working for Jack Faxon. He'd been kind and considerate towards me when they were what I needed most. But I'd had the offer of a move I was helpless to resist. I was now co-editing a small but ambitious film magazine that was more in tune with my interests than Battenberg cakes and sticky buns.

Wages were paid "in bacon butties" they said, but they didn't mind my freelancing a bit when things went quiet, as happened occasionally, so the arrangement made sense.

Mel, still in her job with our old employers, had shown energy and natural organisation skills, which had earned her two good promotions. God, I was so proud of her. So, by the way, was her dad, who had mellowed significantly. He even joined us for the occasional pub lunch.

We were making, Mel and I, just about enough to eat and pay the bills, including the rent on one small chunk of a not-too-dilapidated terrace. As for chilly nights, we had our own cost-free ways of keeping warm.

My job at "Frame", the film magazine, was described as co-editor. It involved all manner of dogsbody duties, from showing the flag at previews to sub-editing contributors' articles. It was also my job to keep on top of correspondence (a chore that the editor hated) and turning press releases into printable stories.

Then there were the evening screenings. It was the only way to keep up with the stream – the torrent, rather - of films submitted for review. We had our own projection room, or what passed for one, with its venerable 16mm projector made by the Bell & Howell Company of Chicago. I liked to think it had rolled off the production line at the time of the US National Defence Education Act, when Franklin D or Harry Truman was US President and Keynesian economics were changing the world.

There was one other item in the projection room: a none-too-comfortable (actually, bloody uncomfortable) single divan. It had saved lives, even the occasional marriage, when screenings ran late but the buses and trains didn't.

It was no problem for Mel and me. She would often come over on the Tube after her work finished, bringing rations with her, and then we'd watch the films together. With some of the stuff that was sent in, two heads were definitely better than one.

We'd kip for the night on the lumpy divan, then go for whatever breakfast we could find the next morning. They knew us well in the local coffee shops.

We were intensely happy. It was an eccentric kind of lifestyle, more suited to Hemingway's Paris than modern London, we liked to tell ourselves. The truth was, we didn't really "do" conventional. We had no interest in changing things.

We'd replaced our lonely childhoods with a self-sufficient, loving relationship. Self-sufficient times two, you could say, which made all the difference.

# CHAPTER 2

AT ONE TIME, I would have worried about mum, still living with the old monster at home, but I'd taken steps to defuse that situation - once and for all, I hoped.

Just to test the water, I'd arranged an overnight visit. It had been months since I last showed my face and I felt more than a bit guilty over leaving mum to it. I still didn't trust my father, even though most of the old conflicts had been about me. Just my moving out should have been enough to take the heat out of things, but you could never rely on it. The only certainties were periodic outbreaks of marital violence.

When you've been brought up in an environment of blows, screams and yelling, you grow antennae that vibrate and glow at the merest suggestion of cruelty and hurt.

From the moment I arrived, I could sense something wasn't quite right. Something throbs in your ears, even though there may be no sound. You can almost feel it on your skin.

I could feel it then. There was impending violence in the air. Couldn't someone invent a barometer that detected these outbursts?

I'd missed the preamble, it seemed, but it looked and felt like I'd arrived at a critical moment. God only knew what had been going on.

Predictably enough, but without any real warning, he blew. He couldn't help himself, which may have been sad for him, but he wasn't my priority. My concern was for mum. How on earth had she put up with him so long?

When he made a move towards her, I stepped into the space between them.

"Get out of the way," he threatened. Master of his own domain.

I looked him defiantly in the eyes. "You mean, out of the way so you can hit her?" I shook my head. "Is that what you want to do, you sad old bugger? Hit her? I'll tell you what, if you want to do any hitting, hit me instead."

He didn't move. He didn't speak. He wasn't used to being challenged.

"Hit me instead, go on. Then I'll hit you back, father or no father. I hope you like the taste of blood. A bloody coward is what you are, only good at hitting women and little boys. But this little boy isn't going to put up with it any longer. It's up to you."

He still said nothing, green around the gills as they say. A good moment to rub it in.

"And don't try to take it out on mum like you usually do. Not now or any other time. Because if you do, I'll be straight back with a couple of my rugby pals, and we'll really sort you out, I promise."

I took mum round to her sister Jazz for the night, then managed to find a B&B, which was lucky in view of how late it was.

As I knew it would be, the truth was he remained the same nasty piece of work he'd always been. It had me thinking. Perhaps there was a way we could put a stop to him.

My solicitor, Mr Lucas, had listened when I spelled out the brutalities that had been inflicted on mum and me, almost week-in, week-out, since the end of the war. He had sat there taking a shorthand note throughout. He wasn't wholly sure whether our account could be treated as formal evidence at my trial (see "Little Boy Bruised"). He rather thought not; but, in his view, it was clearly relevant. He would ensure, he said, that the trial judge was brought up to speed.

I had seen the defence lawyer hand the file to the clerk; then seen the clerk place it before the judge. After taking his time to look it over, this eminent jurist - frighteningly eminent, as it seemed - looked at me just a shade more benignly and passed down a lenient sentence of two years' probation.

That same document was now under lock and key in Mr. Lucas's safe. I'd seen to that. My father didn't even know it existed. But it was enough, if ever he harmed mum, to see him locked up where he belonged.

And if he hadn't known about it before, I made sure he did now.

# CHAPTER 3

AT LAST I'd snuffed out my father's fire. With luck, the only fingers he'd burn now would be his own. And jolly good luck with that. There would be plenty of flames where he was headed.

When I got home, Mel was looking beautiful. Something appetising was simmering on the stove. A bottle of wine stood opened on the table. And my beautiful girl smelled every bit as edible.

"Are you ready to eat?" she asked, dewy eyed and lovely. There was a quandary, for a start.

"There's a question. One dish I'm always ready for," this breathed softly into her ear as though the whole world were eavesdropping.

I received a love punch to the shoulder. "I'll keep," she said. "The dinner won't. Come and eat and tell me how beautiful I look...Then we can come to bed and you can eat me...How does that sound?"

Instant capitulation. Total surrender. "How on earth did I find you?"

"You didn't. Well, you did. You found me in the tea cupboard. Are you happy with what you found?"

"Do you know," I breathed again into her ear, "the moment I opened that door and set eyes on you, I knew my searching days were over. Your eyes were flashing, your hair was shining and, oh boy, were you feisty! I couldn't look away. When I asked you to come out with me, if you'd said no... well, I'd have just had to carry on asking till you changed your mind!"

"When did I ever say no?" There was no answer to that. How did I ever get so lucky? There was no answer to that either.

In bed, bare and beautiful, she wriggled like a fish till I wrestled her still, whereupon she wrapped her arms and legs around me and began kissing me ardently with both her wet places. She was as utterly shameless as only a loving and well-loved partner can be. I adored her. I adored her wetness on my body. I wanted to lap up her wetness.

"I want to eat you," I said.

"You shall." And she clambered on top of me, lowering that sweet pussy right over my mouth, where my tongue lay in wait, ready to lick and stab. Her juices overran me, my cheeks, my chin, my neck, my ears. Who after this would ever search for Paradise? Or doubt that they had already found it? I drank from the well of happiness. As I did, she shuddered, she moaned, shuddered some more, then came again. More floods of joy.

Finally, she was wriggling off my face, wriggling down my body and placing herself above my cock. "Now fuck me," she said.

I was more than eager. So much more than eager. Cock wanted cunt. Cunt wanted cock. It was a meeting of equals. Cunt clasped cock, squeezed cock, cock reached the point of no return... and delivered.

Cut camera. Collapse in gasps and giggles.

"G'night, sweetheart."

"G'night, baby...you know we forgot to wash the dishes..."

"Bugger the dishes."

# CHAPTER 4

OUT OF THE VIE EN ROSE, I'm suddenly stricken with guilt. My relationship with Mel, our relationship with each other, had so quickly become the rails on which ran both our lives, I had never come clean about the dark secret of my past.

Half of me was saying "Why worry? Mel loves you. It doesn't change anything."

The other half: "If you're so sure, how come you've never told her?"

The answer was inevitable. I couldn't bring myself to risk this wonderful happening that had enveloped both our lives. The relationship we shared was the most precious thing I had ever known.

But was it founded on a falsehood? Or at best a half-truth? The answer was yes.

And supposing we stayed together for the rest of our lives? Would it still be there, hidden beneath layers of scar tissue, maybe even starting to fester? What then?

Had I let it get too far already? Would the truth hurt Mel as much as it would hurt me? Did I have any right to hurt her at all? Ridiculous question.

The quandary dominated my thinking, affecting my concentration and my work. It had to be tackled. This was the real payback time, not the hours I had spent in fruitless discussions with Mr Dullard, my probation officer. (See again "Little Boy Bruised".)

As sometimes happens, however, whilst I was looking to choose the moment, the moment chose me.

I'd had a call from Aggi. They were planning a girls' and boys' night out. Would I come? Would Mel come? Would I like to meet up for a chat about it, throw in any ideas?

Three times yes. I'd never been good at saying no to Aggi. I still remembered that first kiss. The day I grew up. And then there was the famous conspiracy. No longer did I indulge lurid fantasies about her, but I always enjoyed talking to her when the opportunity arose.

Here was one of those times.

Then I stopped. Could I truly tap her for some words of wisdom about the problem preying on my mind? The woman's angle. But she wouldn't even know what the problem was. Or would she?

Oh, what the hell, I told myself. I'd enjoy a chat with Aggi.

We met a couple of evenings later, at a cheerful pub in Holborn. She'd had an Eton crop, which suited her. Yes, we did kiss, but there was nothing X-certificate about this one. It was a routine buss, cleared for public performance. She did smell nice, though.

"Drink?" I said.

She'd have a Dubonnet and lemonade, she smiled. Then, "You've been quiet," she said. "I was beginning to think you'd gone off me."

"Ever go off you? You rescued me...from what, I'm not quite sure, but you definitely rescued me."

"From your own self...Isn't that the classic answer?"

"Possibly..."

"I didn't rescue you. You just got on with growing up. Perhaps I helped a little bit."

"A big bit actually."

"I enjoyed it too, you know."

"Stop. Don't say stuff like that to me or I won't be able to...

"Able to what, Bernie?" She didn't change.

"Listen Aggi, I've got a problem."

A sip from her glass, then she focused those warm brown eyes on me.

"Mel and I have been together the best part of two years now. Best's the word. We're almost a married couple. But in all that time, I've never owned up to her about how I came to be working for Jack Faxon in the first place. Do you know the story?"

"Would it matter if I did?"

"Oh, Aggi, no. You I'd trust with my life, same as I would trust Mel. But I feel so guilty. It's as though I felt I couldn't tell her. The risk has always frightened me. If I lost her, I don't I don't know what I'd do."

"Okay, shut up a minute and let Auntie Aggi talk. Do you believe Mel trusts you?"

"Yeah," I nodded.

"Yet you don't trust her. I mean, look at it this way. I'll tell you now. I've known all about it since you came to work for us. Yes, I know, Jack and the chairman were supposed to be the only ones, but I had to know. I have to know just about everything. That's my job.

"So in a way," she went on, "you're saying you trust me more than you trust Mel. I don't think she'd like to hear that, do you?" She didn't wait for an answer. "She loves you, you daft bugger. I'll tell you what I think, shall I? It may not be what you were hoping to hear, but I'll tell you.

"I don't think it matters nearly as much as you imagine. If she ever found out...and it's a pretty big if - I mean, you're not Crippen or one of the Moors murderers - do you really think she'd walk away from you?

"She loves *you*. The same Bernie sitting with me, here, now. So stop worrying. Tell her or don't tell her. You're much more important to her than any of this.

"Now," she said, sitting back. "About this girls' and boy's get-together. You'll both come, won't you? We thought we might do a deal with one of the hotels that's got a pool. We could all swim, eat, drink, dance in the disco and then not have to worry about travelling home."

"Sounds brilliant. We wouldn't miss that."

"Oh, and I forgot to tell you," Aggi grinned. "The chairman's picking up the bill. For everybody!"

"Good god!"

"Yeah, that's what I thought."

"Hey," I interrupted. "Will Woody be coming?"

"Says she will."

"Hey, Aggi," I said, "if she's definitely coming, are you going to make her a white terry-cloth bikini?"

"Just for that, just for that...."

I put my fingers in my ears and stuck out my tongue.

# CHAPTER 5

I wanted to do something really special for Mel, something for her birthday. A long weekend away would make the perfect treat, I thought, and it so happened that the ideal opportunity arose out of nowhere.

Not quite out of nowhere, actually. It came courtesy of one of the big oil companies. They were having a very seductive PR film made in the West of Ireland. Would "Frame" care to do a background piece?

"Exclusive and all bills paid?"

The editor, my boss, would be away covering a documentary film festival in Berlin, I told them, but his associate co- editor would be delighted, so long as he could bring his glamorous PA with him: to field any redirected telephone calls, pass messages, and any other important stuff while her talented boss was absorbing the local colour. And the local liquor, of course.

No messing. It was a "jolly", pure and simple. Associate editors were very rarely first in line for these jamborees. My oil man was delighted and happy to look after the arrangements. "Jerry," I smiled at him over the phone - all the experts say a smile can be heard - "something tells me you're looking for a big splash in the magazine. I won't let you down."

"Never thought for a moment that you might. While the cat's away and all that..."

"Did you know my boss was going to be in Berlin by any chance?" I asked, still smiling.

"You mean, did a little bird whisper..." he smiled back. "There might have been a tiny cheep..."

"If there's any comeback, I'll rely on you to explain how you used your special persuasive powers..."

"Did you ever doubt it?"

All of which explains how Mel and I came to be taking lunch at the Old Ground Hotel, Co. Clare, where Jerry had booked us. I won't say we felt quite like millionaires, but not so very far off. There seemed to be a profusion of wealthy Americans on golfing holidays, or fishing ditto, and one older Irish gentleman taking lunch by himself.

"He keeps smiling at me," Mel said.

"I'm not surprised," I whispered. (Nor was I.) No messing, she looked absolutely good enough to eat. Exactly the gorgeous and feisty young woman I'd rescued from the famous tea-cupboard.

"He's all by himself," she whispered. I knew where this was leading. When it came to stray cats, sad looking dogs, injured birds and now, apparently, lonely Irish pensioners, Mel was a very beautiful and compassionate St Frances. (My spelling is impeccable, by the way.) Then she returned his smile.

"Do you want to invite him over?" I mimed. There were two spare settings at our table.

"You go," she said.

Could I ever refuse her anything? And looking the way she did?

I soft-shoed over to his table. He looked up, possibly a little disconcerted. "Sorry to disturb your lunch," I said to him. "My wife was wondering if you might care to join us. There are two spare settings at our table. We'd really enjoy your company." His smile was, well, the cliché "beguiling" is the only word.

"What a charming thought, I'd be delighted. Eating by one's self is one of those prices one pays for living too long."

An observant waiter, taking note of our negotiations, appeared like magic to help rearrange things. And that was how we came to meet the resident organist and choir-master of... sadly, I can't remember the name of the town, only that it was on the coast in Co. Mayo.

He was a charmer. Conversation somehow became self-propelled. He was a natural lubricant. Oh, and didn't he just have eyes for Mel? She, my cheeky girl, didn't discourage him. Nor did I want her to. If he were of a mind to dream, let him dream. Mel had that kind of effect on people.

We split the last of the wine three ways, I treated him to a cognac and, by the time we were leaving, he had invited us to visit him at his home in Mayo and stay a couple of nights on our way home.

I'm ashamed to say we never got around to it. Mel was beginning to suspect his motives. "Well, you do hear of such things," she kept whispering. We'd only known him half an hour, and that in her bookreally wasn't knowing someone at all.

We motored down through Tralee and eventually caught up with Jerry on the Ring of Kerry. It may have been the wine. Mel began singing about Jerry on the Ring of Kerry, Jerry on the Ring of Kerry" which so much amused her, she kept going back to it till I told her simple things pleased simple minds and she punched me on the shoulder. It wasn't a serious punch but just enough to let me know not to call her simple: not ever. Then we kissed, though there was nothing whatsoever to make up.

Predictably, Jerry was installed in a wayside hostelry which had a couple of movie people's cars pulled up on the adjoining verge. Funny how you can always recognise them. Apart from Jerry propping up the bar, however, there seemed little enough going on.

"Have you eaten?" he wanted to know. We assured him we had. "Then come and get a drink and I'll start filling you in on what's happened. Or, more precisely, what isn't happening yet."

As usual, things were running late. It didn't look much like anything was running at all. Jerry and the producer were still looking at locations. There were also script changes. An alarm bell began tinkling in my brain.

"To put it bluntly" – a great man, Jerry, for being blunt – "there's bugger-all to see. But what it does mean is that I've got you all to myself. I can give you a heads-up on the project, explain what we're looking to do, and at least you can get your thinking cap on.

"Other than that, enjoy yourselves. Your hotel bill is paid till tomorrow night. Now make yourselves comfortable. Lovely to meet you, Mel. You're looking gorgeous by the way. Would you like to star in a film?"

"Sorry, Jerry, I only sleep with Bernie," she told him sweetly. "Nothing personal."

"Isn't it always the way?

"Right. The film. We don't yet have a title and we're still waiting for a revised shooting script, but they'll come along. What I can give you, though, is some background.

"Supposing I was to say to you, a beautiful white Jag, a big truck, a beautiful blonde and the kookiest little kid you've ever seen..."

"Jesus Christ, Jerry," I said. "You're not looking to remake *The Tortoise and the Hare*? Please tell me you're not. That was a total one-off. You'd stand more chance trying to rip off *Casablanca*."

"Thank you, Bernie. My sentiments exactly. Now do you understand why I've got you here at such huge expense?" He drew out those last three words.

"My management have it in their heads that *The Tortoise* is the best road film ever made. Yeah, I know, I know, so who's ever heard of *The Wages of Fear*? But the fact is they've seen *The Tortoise* and they want to create something that kind of, kind of - makes an audience feel the same way. Are you with me so far?"

"So far, Jerry, not so fucking good." It came out more like a growl than I'd intended.

"Okay. So here's why I really wanted to talk to you. You and your boss man at the magazine have to know more movies like this than anyone else on the planet. Now, as it happens... your rather straight-laced boss is, well, too..."

"Honest?" I offered. "Politically correct? He's a lifelong Labour voter, you know...

"Did I even hint?" He tried to look a little hurt...but it didn't wash. He hefted his shoulders till they were massaging his ears. "But I'm sure you get the drift, don't you?"

I was beginning to.

"So what do you reckon?" His eyes were fixed on mine and our noses were almost shaking hands.

They say people swallow hard in moments like these. I did.

"Never mind about shooting a film, Jerry, I think I want to shoot myself..."

"Men of honour," he muttered. "What's wrong with money, all of a sudden?"

"When you put it like that..."

"I do. So, are you on board or not?"

I could smell the money. The down payment on a nice family house. For a nice little family. Persuasive imagery, too.

"Okay, Jerry." I was beginning to build the part. "Here's the deal."

And I spelled it out to him. "This isn't the kind of thing you can plan out on the back of an envelope. Just look where that got Dave Cameron."

"Dave who?"

"Never mind. Give me a week to do some digging and thinking. I'll get back to you. But no promises, I'm not even sure this can be done. When I need to get back to you, your office will have to hook us up. I can't just come steaming over here again."

"Okay."

"And, naturally, we'll have to talk about a fee."

He didn't blink. That's oil men for you.

# CHAPTER 6

Mel looked at me like she'd just discovered she was about to marry a *mafioso*. "Okay, I listened," she said, "I listened to every word. But what Jerry's suggesting - is it even legal?"

Those blue eyes of hers were pinning me to the driving seat.

"It's perfectly legal, so long as we don't do anything... *ill*egal..."

"You mean as long as we don't get caught." She could be very sarcastic when she wanted. It looked like this was going to be one of those times. "And can we please drop the George Raft impersonation?" Actually, I was more impressed by the first-person plural. That's my girl.

"Okay. First of all, we haven't done anything yet except talk. Obviously, we won't suggest anything that might lead to a breach of copyright. I'm not that daft. And I'm sure their lawyers aren't daft either.

"Maybe it's a non-starter. But look! We've had - we're still having - a lovely weekend on the back of it. And there may even be a workable solution, in which case we'll make some money. But no promises, as I told Jerry, it's a difficult one."

"I don't want to be visiting you in - where is it, Pentonville?"

"Stop worrying. That's where they used to put the hard cases. I'm not sure it's even there any more." I started to laugh, until I noticed actual tears welling up in her eyes.

"Well, *I don't,*" *she* said again. "Not even in Brixton."

The tears were now rolling down her cheeks. I was on the ropes. All I could do was dry her eyes and kiss her lips. She kissed me back, a bit half-heartedly.

"Listen," I said, her wet cheeks now held gently between my palms. "We can walk away from this. We can walk away from it now, if you like. Supposing we give it just a couple of days' thought when we get home? We might even have a brainwave. If we don't, I'll get back to Jerry and tell him it can't be done. Is that better?"

Mel nodded. I was kissed again. This time, a much better kiss.

That night in bed, Mel was particularly loving, as though she just couldn't get close enough to me. It was like being a single, conjoined human rather than two people making love. I had never felt closer, more absorbed, more part of this amazing young woman who had become an irreplaceable part of my life. She didn't have to tell me she felt the same about me. I could sense it in every fibre of my body. And every delicious fibre of hers.

To be so loved was like an epiphany for someone who, for so many years, had felt little but torment and the guilt of loveless acts of pleasure. Or to put it in plainer language, I felt I had re-joined the human race and the human race, in the shape of my beautiful partner, had taken me to its heart again. And between its delectable thighs.

I slept the sleep of the forgiven. I awoke feeling cleansed.

*********

Cleansed, but not entirely untroubled. Knocking on my door came two unresolved issues. The secret I still kept unconfessed. And, a more practical consideration: if we continued our loving with such abandon as the previous night, we ought to look again at wedding plans.

We sorted both over a long, leisurely breakfast.

While Mel was dabbing marmalade off my chin, I took the plunge. "You'll soon be 21, my sweetheart. I don't suppose you feel like marrying me?"

"And I thought I was going to end up having to ask you..."

"I'm asking now. You know how hugely much I love you."

"Hugely much? I like that. Have you never thought how 'hugely much' I love you back?"

"Is that a 'yes' then?"

"No, it's a 'Yes, please!' Please, very much, I do want you to marry me!"

"You mean like marrying each other?"

"You cotton on quite quickly when you work at it," her eyes were gleaming now.

"There's just one thing I've never told you."

"Something bad?"

"Depends how you look at it..."

"Here we go then. Just nod or shake your head."

"Have you ever murdered anyone? Have you ever mugged an old lady? I think I'd know if you'd ever robbed a bank...

"Have you ever interfered with little kids? Have you ever stolen a charity box? Have you ever been cruel to animals? No, I didn't think so. You'll have to help, I'm running out of ideas here..."

"When I was in my teens, long before I knew you, I had a torrid affair with a scoutmaster."

She literally fell about laughing. "Oh, my God...Is that it? Were you in love with him?"

"I don't think so." That, I decided, was confession enough.

"Okay," she said. "Thanks for telling me. Just don't invite him to our wedding!"

By the end of breakfast, after about the third cup of coffee - each, that is - my personal sky had cleared to a brilliant azure. Mel really wasn't impressed. It had been as easy as Aggi had predicted. We'd been living together now for nearly two years. It was as if she knew as much about me and my dubious past as she cared to know.

"You do still want to marry me, not your sexy scoutmaster?"

"What do you think." It wasn't a question.

"Thank god for that, I was beginning to fear the worst."

In those days, you had to be 21 to get married, unless you eloped over the border to Gretna Green, where 16 was old enough. But seeing Mel and I had been living together since I was 18 and she was only a slightly illegal 17, we decided it wasn't worth the effort.

What was very important was the month you chose to tie the knot. If you picked the last month of the tax year, the Revenue refunded all that year's income tax. You can imagine how that boosted the number of March weddings. Nowadays it's all changed. They probably make you pay more.

No panic, anyway. There was a lot still to be thought about. Like who did we dare invite to the wedding? And how much did my sweet bride-to-be know about George Raft?

# CHAPTER 7

The girls' and boys' night out was fraught with danger. Booze, bosses, bosoms, bottoms, bikinis, a lethal combination more suited to a Club 18-30 beach party than a firm's do. People never learn.

Mel and I found ourselves a quiet corner where we hoped we'd be well out of it. No such luck. They came and found us. Were we living in sin? It depended what you meant by sin. Could I get hold of the latest porno movies? I didn't know which the latest ones were. And we didn't get that kind of thing sent in for review?

What none at all? Not even that *Breathless*? French film, original title *A bout de souffle*, did you mean? Wonderful New Wave movie - Jean-Paul Belmondo, Jean Seberg. Not a whiff of sex unless you like to fantasise about Seberg's tiny tits, not that you ever get to see them. You have to fantasise, you see.

Wasn't that Seberg married to Frank Sinatra? No, you've got it wrong, he was married to Mia Farrow. What's the difference, she didn't have tits either? Now Ava Gardner, she was married to Frank, she *did* have tits.

"Everybody having a good time?" This was the chairman, our benefactor, thrower of the party. Must have been a good year.

"We were just discussing Frank Sinatra's wives and which of them had the biggest tits."

Chairman looks pensive for a moment. "I'd say Ava Gardner, definitely."

"What about Mia Farrow?"

"Mia Farrow never had any tits." Authoritative voice of the chairman."No tits at all. A boy, if you ask me."

"We'll defer to your judgment, chairman."

"Bloody well better had. Who's going to get me another large Remy Martin... Don't all rush at once, will you?"

It's Jack Faxon who scurries off to the bar for the chairman's treble cognac. The chairman still has the floor as they say. "Somebody tell me, why are all these waitresses still wearing their knickers? I thought it had all been arranged." He makes a play of sniffing his fingers.

Across the room, Mel and Bernie have now been joined by Aggi. Bernie looks at Aggi, "Glad you came, Aggs?" *Stage direction: If you notice Bernie has slipped into the 3rd person, you're not mistaken. Unsurprisingly, he's feeling a bit out of it, product of booze and boredom. It's a party that wants to be an orgy but doesn't know how.*

This is me again. I'd like to suggest that Mel and I, and Aggs if she feels like it, slip away before the waitresses get deprived of their knick-knacks. I'm not certain either of the girls heard me. Or even if I spoke. They're sitting huddled in the corner, and they're either whispering or canoodling. Hard to tell with girls, sometimes.

Aggs still hasn't told me if she's glad she came. If she did, I didn't notice it happening. (Sorry!) She pulls a bit of a "Yuk" face, which I hope is meant for the party, not for me personally.

Then we're all three in a taxi. Then out of the taxi and I'm fishing for money to pay the driver. We negotiate a flight of stairs and there's our own front door, Mel's and mine, and Mel lets us in. Like clockwork.

What an escape. What an awful party. And what's supposed to have happened to the swimming? Or did I miss that? Probably just as well. Woody in a bikini would be too much for my long-suffering constitution.

"Right, who's going to make coffee?" Am I talking to myself? We all need coffee. "It's all right. I'll go, I'm not as drunk as all that. Promise."

*Am I* on a promise? They're giggling again. Maybe it's just them sharing a promise.

"Mel," I said, "have we ever thanked Aggs for being such a brilliant match-maker? Match-maker, conspirator...call it what you like. Do you suppose we'd be sitting here now if it wasn't for our Aggi?

"All right, I'm a conspiracy theorist. Better than that. I'm a grateful conspiracy theorist. You and I," I said, looking at Mel, "...you and I owe a debt of gratitude to Aggi for recognising us as the star-crossed lovers of the second floor. Romeover and Juliet." Giggle? Apparently not.

"I'm wasted," I tell them.

"You're telling us," says Aggs.

And I thought I had my audience. The giggling had stopped. They were actually waiting for me to go on. Not a muscle moved, not an eyelid twitched. (Not unlike the burial of Sir John Moore at Corunna, an inner voice tells me.) They were waiting for me.

"A debt of gratitude, yeah. So what I am about to suggest...is we repay that debt of love, with the only currency we've got ...More love! "

"Come to bed with us, Aggs. Come to bed with us and let's seal the bond. We three against the world!"

By this time, I noticed, they were holding hands – and the giggling had started again. Or was it tickling? Or both?

"Pretty please..." I added. "Pretty, pretty please." I stopped talking. I might have been swaying. My eyes followed the girls.

The girls looked at each other. Aggi's eyebrows made two arches. Mel's followed suit. They looked at each other, said something to each other that I wasn't meant to hear. Then trotted off to the bedroom holding hands.

Giggling came next. Quite a lot of girlish giggling. Lovely sound.

I closed my eyes and let them have their giggles. Yes. such a lovely, happy sound. They didn't need me.

A tense few minutes later, when giggles became sounds of shared pleasure, I had to peek. They were tribbing. Slowly and painstakingly. Making the most of every moment and every movement. And they didn't need me.

I slipped back into the sitting room, returned to my chair and nodded off.

Happy. Yes, happy. That was how I felt. And, just for the moment, I didn't need them.

# CHAPTER 8

At the office next morning - well, same morning actually - and somewhat bleary eyed, I was putting together my first solo edition of "Frame". My editor, Brian, had been in touch to make sure I hadn't burned the office down and seemed confident enough to let me sink or swim. Preferably swim, he said.

In Berlin, he had a girlfriend, Frieda, who was the hottest number since Lilli Marlene apparently, and he wanted to spend a few more days with her. I'd seen pictures of Frieda and couldn't say I blamed him.

*"Falling in love again, never wanted to..."*

In between times, I'd been trying to get my head around Jerry's problem. Now mine as well, of course, except I hadn't entirely committed myself. There was still wriggle room. If I couldn't come up with a clever wheeze of some kind, which is what he really wanted, then he'd have to paddle his own canoe. I didn't have the time, nor that kind of talent if I'm honest, to create an original treatment of my own. *The Tortoise* had been an absolute one-off masterpiece.

I could always lie; I was quite good at that. Tell him I was still burrowing away in the archives, but that it was turning out every bit as difficult as I'd predicted. What he really needed was a top-notch, brilliant screenwriter – who would want MONEY (my upper-case letters, by the way) – just to come up with an equally brilliant treatment.

That analysis, in its own way, was also brilliant. Or so I told myself. Question was, who was going to tell Jerry?

The simplest answer is nearly always the best: Mel.

"You're a rat," she told me over dinner that night. Which, incidentally, I'd prepared, even though I knew she'd see this for the subterfuge it was. "Anyway, what am I expected to tell him?"

"Don't know yet. Well, I've got an idea. Tell him it can't be done."

"Just like that?"

"Er...Yeah." I didn't think she'd kill me. We'd been talking about getting married, even about babies. Even my murderous father hadn't managed to kill me, though he'd had a few good tries. "We'll come up with something," I offered.

"You'd better," she said.

"Fancy an early night?"

"Uh, uh...Think of all that good thinking time going to waste."

# CHAPTER 9

Have you ever thought about germination?

A seed falls to the ground. It rolls around in the mud for a while till some great, hoofing boot comes along and pushes it down into the soft, welcoming soil. Then comes this huge lump of a dog and pisses all over the very same spot. The piss is warm and the seed quite likes this mud and piss combination, which coats it all over.

After a long while, the seed thinks to itself, "It's getting warm down here, I wonder if spring could be on its way," and it notices that the layer of mud and piss is wearing a bit thin in places and the moisture is finding its way into the seed's private parts. Did seeds have private parts? I wasn't sure. But anyway...

The seed starts feeling sexy and before it knows what's happening, there's all these roots and stalks popping out from here, there and everywhere...

Such a wonder of nature is taking place right now inside Bernie's brain. A tiny seed of an idea is germinating in that warm, mushy receptacle. An idea that in due course may develop into a runner bean, a lupin, a foxglove, a hollyhock, a michaelmas daisy or even a treatment for an award-winning promotional film.

A film, mark you, which will have no recourse whatever to white Jaguars, beautiful blonde models, kooky kiddies or songs sung by the Spencer Davis Group.

While Mel sleeps the sleep of the just off the hook - not that she yet knows it - Bernie waters the seed with the liquid manure of his fertile imagination and, little by little, there emerges the story of a handsome American from Boston who looks just a little like Clark Gable. Who flies to Shannon Airport with his beautiful, sporty wife (just a hint of Vivian Leigh). What beckons them is the golfing holiday of a lifetime; but, alas, it's his fishing tackle that's been shipped instead of his clubs!

But fear not. Three thousand miles away, his clubs and his sporty wife's fishing poles are on their way to the airport to catch the first flight to the Emerald Isle and, by next morning, everything is safely delivered. CUT TO the golfing *and* coarse fishing holiday of their dreams, made even more fabulous, of course, by the luxury of the shiny sedan that was ready and waiting for them.

We know, of course, it's only an outline treatment. But garish enough to satisfy most tastes. Someone else will have to put the meat on the bone.

And Mel won't have to kill Bernie after all. Actually, she was only going to ration his bedroom athletics.

There remains, mind you, that first solo edition of "Frame". Seventy-two pages to be filled. Reviews to write. Articles to sub-edit. An editorial think-piece to be thought of. Sounds easy when you put it like that, but there's only half the normal amount of preparation time, and that's nobody's fault but his own. Still, it wouldn't be the first time "Frame" had published three weeks late.

And Brian could hardly complain, lolling around some Berlin boudoir, fucking the shit out of Lilli Marlene.

He should think himself lucky to have a genius like Bernie taking charge. That's what Mel tells Bernie, anyway. And though she doesn't yet know it, she's going to be helping out with the film reviews.

Speaking of which, it could be a long night. There's a Czech feature to watch, a bundle of Russian documentaries – some of them in glorious Sovcolor – and a bunch of experimental films courtesy of the British Film Institute.

*"Message to Mel: Bring extra butties, crisps and drinks. Love and kisses."*

*Bear in mind, all this is 40 years too early for mobile phones and texting. How did we communicate? It wasn't telepathy, we had these big black bakelite things. You must have seen them in old movies. In Hollywood movies, the black things were often white. Not that that made much difference.*

*Before we thread up the old Bell & Howell 601 projector, let me just ask you. Do you really want to watch the films with us? The Czech feature is probably good, they often are. But the Russian documentaries are pretty dire as a rule and the experimental films are a mixed lot. Sometimes rude, sometimes just weird.*

*Don't want to bother? Something better on telly? Suit yourselves.*

Dutifully, Mel and I sit through the pile of movies, all pretty much as expected – except for the feature, actually

Polish, which has the title "Ashes and Diamonds". As film buffs now know, it will soon become recognised as one of the great movies of the 20<sup>th</sup> Century and its male lead, Zbigniew Cybulski, will be pronounced an international love idol.

Europe's answer to Jimmy Dean.

Died terribly young, like Jimmy. Don't they say the best ones always do?

I have no record of what I wrote in my review. I may have cribbed from Barry Norman or Penelope Lively. Those who know me well wouldn't be shocked. Like Boris Johnson, I've been guilty of worse.

By the time we finish, both Mel and I are bug-eyed. The old divan looks more inviting than it has any right. We stretch out and make ourselves as comfortable as we can by fitting arms and legs around each other and trying to dodge the ferocious bedsprings. It's not cold, so nor are we. But no sex tonight, thank you.

# CHAPTER 10

The following Monday starts like any ordinary Monday but it won't finish that way. As is well known, Cataclysm never books ahead.

I'm in the "Frame" office before 9 o'clock. There's catching up to be done. And Jerry to be let off the hook. I give him a call.

"Jerry, old fruit, I think I may just have solved your movie conundrum. We've got an idea which, with any luck, just might fly." Might as well be positive, I always say. "I've been trawling through the archives like I said I would, but there's nothing there that looks even hopeful, let alone helpful.

"Nothing we can rip off, anyway. That was what you wanted, wasn't it? Something that could be ripped off. Something that would stand the shock, charm the masses, and all without a fat lawyer's letter landing on your doormat. No, not a fat lawyer, a fat envelope!"

I swear he can be very thick at times for an overpaid oil company exec. Or maybe not, I haven't met very many of them.

"Listen, Jerry. It's original, no borrowings. It's got humour, family appeal, even some transatlantic potential." (I was sure I could hear him making some quietly appreciative noises.) "Thought that might appeal to you."

"Yes, transatlantic. That's what I said. But listen, it's only the bare bones of a treatment at the moment. Just one sheet of paper. Something to get your grey cells working around. No, no - you're not risking anything at the moment, except maybe your job if you go for it...

"And stop panicking, will you? I'm joking, for god's sake. Look, we'll fax it to you. Then you can throw in your four pennyworth and we'll see where we go from there... E-mail? Don't be silly. It won't be invented for another forty years. That's right, I'm clairvoyant!

"Okay! Faxing it to your home right now. Not to your office. I must say, Jerry, that sounds highly suspicious to me. Who don't you want to see it?

"Okay, give me the fax number."

Jerry was beginning to worry me. First he entertains Mel and yours truly to an all-paid weekend jaunt to the West of Ireland. Then he wants me to devise a way of ripping off one of the most famous films of its kind in the world. Now he doesn't want the treatment going anywhere near his office. I don't know what he's up to, but I don't see my Jewish momma awarding it her *kosher* seal of approval.

One thing's certain, though, or so I tell myself. If he wants to press ahead to a full treatment, he'll have to find some other mug. For some reason, I just don't smell money at the end of this charade.

All of this is small beer, however, compared to what's just around the corner.

Shortly after 10 a.m. I get a call from the mysterious Brendan Madders, whom I know only as a name. He is reputed to be the founder of "Frame" and is the money behind it. Not that there is all that much money behind it, hence the joke about the bacon buttie wages, but what money there is belongs to Brendan. Only Brian has personal contact with him. But now it's Brendan who is suddenly there on the other end of my telephone.

"Mr. Bravo."

"Speaking."

"May I call you Bernie?"

"By all means. Everybody does..."

"This is Brendan Madders. I need to come in and speak to you on a serious matter. I'll be with you in about thirty minutes."

"Certainly. Are you able to tell me anything now?"

"Better when we meet face to face. I'll see you shortly."

Unsettling, to put it mildly. Why on earth would he want to see me? What have I done? Or what have I not done? Are sins of omission supposed to be better or worse than the other kind?

Has my distant past finally caught up with me? I haven't fiddled the petty cash – apart from the odd pound when we needed to send out for milk. Has he heard about my Irish jolly?

I'm none the wiser when he arrives. A tall, thin-faced man. Sixty-ish, I'd say. We don't have a posh room for posh people, so I settle him in the one comfortable chair, offer him coffee – which he declines – then sit down at my desk and wait for him to speak.

"Bernie," he begins, "or do you prefer Bernard?"

I smile and shrug. "Whichever."

"I wish we were able to meet in more pleasant circumstances. I have to tell you, I think something untoward may have happened to Brian. He's been in Germany, as I'm sure you know."

"For the documentary festival..."

"Exactly. But it finished over a week ago. Since then, not a word. I take it you haven't heard from him either?"

"Not since the day the festival concluded. He phoned that day – I was out and didn't take the call. He said he was staying in Berlin an extra day or two. Visiting a friend there, apparently."

Madders looked thoughtful. "That would be the lovely Frieda, I imagine."

He'd started drumming his nails on the edge of my desk. Brian's desk, I should say. "I rather thought that was all over. They were political allies, you won't be surprised to know. I do hope he wasn't trying to get her out of East Berlin."

"Do you have any contacts?" I asked. "With the Foreign Office, I mean. Or MI6?"

He'd stopped drumming his nails and was looking at me curiously. "Those are very good questions," he said, "and I'm really not sure I should be answering them. Has he ever talked about me?"

"Hardly at all."

"Right," said Madders, shifting himself more upright in the chair. "Leave all that to me. The real reason I'm here is to ask you if you feel confident about running 'Frame' by yourself until, hopefully, he turns up. Though I have to say I'm worried. Not about your professional abilities but about his safety. I always felt his fascination with Frieda was dangerous. She had – maybe still has – some very dubious friends."

He stood up to go. "Did you know I actually founded 'Frame'? I was its first editor. Remember that if you find you need help with anything. I'm very willing."

"I'm very grateful for that, Brendan – may I call you Brendan? I'm sure we'll be fine for the current month, and hopefully our errant friend will be back soon anyway." I made sure I said the "errant friend" bit with a gentle smile. "And you will let me know if you hear anything?"

"Most certainly," he said, and he was gone.

# CHAPTER 11

I'm not sure how long I sat there in silence. I don't think I was dead. Something had taken my breath away, no doubt about that, but I still didn't think I'd expired.

Surely, I should have reacted in some way to Madders's revelation. Panic? Tears? Demented laughter? Astonishment? No, nothing about Brian astonished me any longer. He was just about the most unpredictable person I had ever known – and proud of it too. Being predictable was anathema to him.

I had long grown out of the astonishment phase where he was concerned. Brian was Brian.

But perhaps he wasn't Brian any more. Had that sunk in? Perhaps he wasn't anyone any more. Maybe he was just the deceased.

Then I stopped myself. Would any of this have gone through my mind if it hadn't been for the dark suggestions of Brendan Madders, the Man in Black. Except he hadn't been wearing black. But the very phrase rang a clanking bell in my distant, impressionable past.

I couldn't just do nothing. But for the moment that was exactly what I had to do.

Not strictly true, of course. I had a magazine to edit. To conceive, to plan, to construct from the component parts that presented themselves, including the advertising space that had been sold and any special positions that had been promised and paid for.

Special positions were a *bete-noire* with Brian. No special positions booked without his prior agreement.

I had to stick to the rules. The way my mind was working seemed suddenly to be based on the supposition that he would come striding through the door at any moment, demanding a progress report that I couldn't provide at the drop of a hat, a thought that stimulated the brain cells considerably.

Never mind the sultry Frieda; never mind the mystery surrounding the magazine's errant editor. It was time to start getting the show on the road, or whatever cliche seemed the most appropriate just then.

There were a couple of good articles on over-matter from the previous month and some film reviews still waiting their turn. More reviews were waiting to be written up and a piece on classroom films that was going to need some work. Quite a lot of work actually. Why were so many so-called educationists such graceless, careless writers?

There should of course have been a full report on the Berlin Documentary Festival, but it was anybody's guess when or whether that would ever turn up. No Brian, no report. Three pages allocated that would now need to be filled. Unless I could find a freelancer who'd been there.

I could do a piece myself on the multi-award-winning *Tortoise* and how the automotive sector were falling over each other to come up with something brilliant to emulate its success; but a little voice told me I might not get thanked for it. Which reminded me, I hadn't heard a dickie-bird from Jerry about the suggested treatment. Maybe he hadn't stopped laughing.

So many balls in the air, so many balls-ups just waiting to happen.

On top of all this, I'd been neglecting Mel. God love her, she knew what she was getting into with me, but there were limits. I gave her a quick call. "Shall we go out for a bite, tonight?"

"Mmmmm."

"You're eating your lunch..."

"I am. But I'd love to eat out tonight...Can we afford it?"

"Anything for you, my sweetheart – so long as it's not sole *waleska* at Wheeler's or one of those Japanese steaks at that new kneel-on-the-floor restaurant ..."

"Tell you what," she dived in. "How about our favourite *Trattoria* on Dean Street?"

"Can't think of a nicer idea. Meet over here, then go on together? If we go early, we shouldn't need to book. Can you get here for six?"

"For you, anything. I love you."

"Love you too... As I'll show you tonight."

"Promises." I was being very slightly taken to task.

"Sorry. You can spank me if you like..."

"Not a chance. That would be a reward, not a punishment."

"I'll be good."

"You'd better be. Or I won't spank you again."

"You tie me in knots."

"Now there's an idea."

Oh, Mel. Delight of my life. Whatever it is you're doing to me, I love it.

## Interlude

Being away from Mel, even for a few hours, feels like a lifetime in solitary. I could eat her alive, as I most certainly shall tonight. After all, why should the sisterhood have the monopoly of all the best things in life?

Of all the eating places we used to frequent, the Trattoria Romana was easily our favourite. I'd like to think it's still there, but I'm talking about a lot of years ago. It wasn't just the food. It was the noise, the fun, the laughter. And the food. An entire Mozart opera on a plate. (You didn't think Mozart was Italian? Don't be boring. Nobody wrote superlative Italian opera like Wolfgang Amadeus.)

And to be there, sitting opposite each other, feeding our faces (and each other's), eating and laughing - a deliciously messy combination - was heaven on earth served with *putanesca* sauce and Chianti...

We were so close, united in love, coalesced into one joyous being and far, far more than the sum of our parts.

We were like a mathematician's nightmare: one of those insoluble equations that makes no sense, however long you play with it; a poet's vision of a Xanadu without limits or dimensions.

In the end, you have no alternative but to invent a word for it. If nothing else comes to mind, happy will always suffice. The fact, incidentally, that such sublime happiness is infectious leads to an irresistible chain reaction that lifts everyone on its crest.

As for Mel and Bernie, by the time they'd got around to the second *zabaglione* that always follows the first one, they were perched on the very crest of the crest: perched, poised and ready to name the day.

And no one, no one, was going to stand in their way.

# CHAPTER 12

It was time for a recap.

By some miracle, the forthcoming edition of "Frame" had gone to press and, without blowing my trumpet, it was going to be indistinguishable from those that went before. So far, so good – though I was keeping my fingers crossed about Brendan Madders' reaction when he came to see it.

Of Brian, there was still no news. I have to say, no news has ever proved good news in my experience. I was growing increasingly worried. About him, that is. About "Frame" I wasn't worried. I could handle the magazine, of that I was confident. Just so long as Madders let me get on with it. And as long as he kept paying me, preferably on the same scale as Brian. But that was getting ahead of myself.

For Mel and me it was – how did they put it in those days at Cape Kennedy? – "All Systems Go". We were compatible. We were both working and earning. And, oh yes, we were very much head over heels. Everything was so "hunky dory" as people put it in those days, we even asked ourselves whether it was worth getting married at all; but then I looked into those liquid blue eyes and the reason was right there, painted in letters six feet high.

It wasn't a matter of making an honest woman of her. It was about keeping the happy woman of her. I so wanted that. For both of us. Her face shone whenever we talked about it.

Some of the traditional sticking points didn't even arise. Neither of us could face a church wedding. What price hypocrisy? Register Office for us. Wedding breakfast? Reception? Non-starters. We didn't want to involve either family in splashing out money.

Too uncomfortable by half. It would be tricky enough just having them there. They certainly wouldn't get on. And my father, of course, never got on with anyone.

"Why don't we just invite our friends?" This was Mel.

"Do you think we'd get away with it?"

"Of course. So long as we didn't tell the families it was happening..." This is Mel.

"You're a genius. A very devious genius. You do know I love you more every day?"

"So I should hope." Mel again.

Pause for cuddles, kisses and prolonged love-making on the sofa.

"You do realise," coming up for air, "if we do that, we can forget wedding presents?"

"You're my wedding present," Mel stretching, hands behind her neck, elbows akimbo, principal assets making much of themselves.

"How's that for a coincidence?" Bernie reaching out.

This may give the impression that our minds were never far away from the mechanics of procreation. How right you would be.

What made it so delightfully easy was the fact that Mel had somehow persuaded the nice lady at the Marie Stopes clinic into equipping her with a diaphragm without punching a great hole in it with a pair of scissors – which was standard procedure, apparently, where couples had not yet tied the knot!

Which was all very well. But "Frame" was calling again.

Another edition to be planned. More films to be watched and reviewed. More previews to attend. More articles to be commissioned, more contributors to be winkled out, more writing, more sub-editing, more layouts and proof reading. Not to forget correspondence.

It was flat out all day, every day, and a fair few evenings too. Even when Brian and I had both been working, it had been a full-time occupation, something I'd rather overlooked in my enthusiasm to take on the task.

I'd been loath to ask Madders to get too involved, which I feared might happen, but it did occur to me that he could take on some of the film reviewing. He'd been doing most of it when "Frame" was getting started. He might even enjoy it again. He'd be helping without getting into my hair. I'd see if he could come in for a chat.

He might even have some news of Brian.

# CHAPTER 13

Madders was complimentary about the new issue of "Frame", which was no bad start. His facial expression, however, was fixed somewhere between serious and daunting.

"What news of Brian?" I ventured...

His first response was an intake of breath through lips only partially open. As facial signals go, that's rarely a good sign.

"I'm going to have to take you into my confidence," he began. "You asked me before whether I had any contacts with the powers that be and, as I remember, I rather dodged the question. That probably told you a lot. You weren't just close to the mark, you were actually spot on."

I felt my face change without prompting.

"This doesn't mean I'm about to start divulging state secrets," he smiled. Though briefly enough. "I mustn't forget you're a journalist, after all. But there are bits I can tell you.

"We thought initially, 'we' meaning my colleagues and myself, that there might indeed be a political dimension to his disappearance, but so far nothing of that kind has come to light... Brian came in from the cold a long time ago."

"Came in... from the cold?" the words came slowly. I frowned.

"Now, come on," said Madders, "don't tell me you don't know what that means."

"Not at all. The words just surprised me."

"All right. In any case, there isn't that much more to tell you. We concluded there was no political angle to follow. Everything had moved on so much since Brian's days. So we began looking at the Frieda angle. In other words, could it be a *crime passionelle*? Frieda, from what I know of her, isn't just a very attractive woman. She's an intellectual – Brian's ideal, you might say – and like so many of her type, a rather naughty girl.

"And that, my dear chap, is where things remain. For now, it's a matter for the Berlin police. The reason I'm worried about Brian is that he just might have upset a boyfriend or lover of the lady in the case...in which case he's quite possibly lying in an alley or floating in a canal, waiting for the *Polizei* to discover him. I don't somehow see a ransom note turning up in this case.

"There is one other possibility, I suppose. He could have done a runner, as they say. But that would be very un-Brian."

"Very." I could only agree.

"The moment there's any more news, I'll be in touch. He could yet walk through the door, of course, in which case tell him to contact me pronto."

"Of course, Brandon. Oh, and just before you go, I wonder if you'd let me treat you to lunch at some time. I'd rather like to pick your brains about another matter?"

"By all means, old chap. But let it be my treat. I'm rather an expensive man to feed. Give me a bell and we'll fix something, soon as you like. And don't forget, if you want any help with the magazine, I'm always here."

Could it just be, as Brendan had suggested, that Brian – he of the wandering eye and ever ready dick – had stretched his luck too far for once?

Apart from two wives, he'd had numerous women and never been shy about it. There'd been a ballet dancer when he was just a junior Don Juan in his teens; then an actress, a French interpreter, a German interpreter, a sweet young Jewish journalist; and those were just the ones I knew about.

Had his luck run out? Had he fallen foul of a husband or boyfriend? Could it even be an aggrieved mistress who'd gone after him with a kitchen knife.

Perhaps, one day, we'd find out. But possibly not from his own lips. And could there be just the suggestion of a fault in the weave of my concern? Could his misfortune, if there had been a misfortune, be my stroke of - I didn't want to say it.

Mel saw it in a different light when we talked about it that evening. Luck followed no rules, she assured me. "Good luck, bad luck. You get what you're allocated. It's not as if you ever wished him dead, did you?"

"Not often. Maybe a few times when he rewrote one of my leading articles."

"Not the same thing."

She was my pole-star, my guiding light. My No. 1 supporter.

Kisses, cuddles. And so to bed. (Sorry. No peeping!)

# CHAPTER 14

I was beginning to enjoy Brendan Madders's company. His sense of humour was dry but it was there. You just had to recognise it.

We were enjoying a leisurely lunch at Rule's steak house, Brendan making most of the conversation. I was awaiting my moment but didn't have to wait very long.

"There was something you wanted to talk to me about. I had the impression it may have been something delicate?"

I thanked him for breaking the ice. "There is something, yes. Something I hope you might be able to help me with.

"It goes back to when we had our first conversation about Brian, when I rather indelicately asked you if you had any connections with, er, the people who know things..."

"People who know things?"

You don't often run across chucklers these days, but Madders was a definite chuckler. It's a very subtle form of communication. He was quietly chuckling now.

"The kinds of people," I went on, "who know where to look for answers. Answers to obscure questions like

'What on earth was my father up to during the war?' – that sort of thing. I can't ask him, because we're barely on speaking terms, and I'm sure he wouldn't tell me anyway."

"Your father?" Madders raised his eyebrows heavenwards. "Why should I know anything about your father? If I ever met the man, I certainly wouldn't have been aware of it." How wrong can a man be?

"Let me start at the beginning, Brendan," I said. "It was always believed that my father served in the Royal Air Force during the war. I've even seen photographs showing him in his uniform. He was stationed in Egypt, somewhere in the Canal Zone, at a place called Shalufa.

"He was an Aircraftsman pure and simple, you might say, but truly not as simple as all that. He was actually a rare breed, a wireless operator or radio technician, I don't really know which – or even if there was a difference. Be that as it may, the RAF were so short of them, he was drafted willy-nilly out of the merchant navy in 1940 and told he was now an airman.

"Lucky for him, as it happened, because his ship was torpedoed next time out and only three survived. As was usually the case, the wireless operator wasn't one of them. You probably know, they stayed at their position dotting and dashing until the water reached the set.

"I only really got interested in my father's war service much later, when I got over my gruesome childhood with him, and decided to start digging. As far as I was aware, he'd had what my artillery-man uncle – a veteran of Monte Cassino – had always called a "good" war. Less blood and guts, I assumed, was what he meant by that.

"But something must have happened. Something sufficiently traumatic to have turned him into – well, frankly, an unbalanced, even potentially murderous lunatic who couldn't keep his hands and fists off me or my mother." That was what was driving me mad.

"As I say, I started digging anywhere I could. I found all kinds of records, pretty well everything that the Air Ministry had chosen to make public. I even found lists of personnel who had served where he did, or supposedly did, at RAF Shalufa in Egypt.

"But nothing. There was no trace of him. It was as though the RAF had lost him, forgotten him or maybe even disowned him. None of which seemed very likely.

"I even wrote to the Air Ministry asking for any information they could provide. I said I was preparing an anniversary album to present to him. It was a very long shot, needless to say, and it won't surprise you to hear they weren't awfully helpful.

"What I would dearly love to know is... what on earth could have led them to expunge him from their records, turn him into a non-Airman as it were. It has to have been something serious, surely?"

For what seemed a long time, Brendan Madders didn't move or speak. I even wondered if he had dozed off. But no; I was doing him an injustice.

"Fascinating," he murmured. "Intriguing, yes. You're right in one way. Something certainly doesn't add up. There are things that might have led to the situation you've been describing, but extremely rare, I would think. Maybe not quite so rare in wartime, especially where it concerns a rare bird like your father.

"What matters most during a war is winning it, and I'm sure rules have been known – or *not* known, you might say – to be bent a little for the good of the cause.

"I suppose you're wondering if I can call in a favour from one of the 'people who know things', as you delicately put it. I'm going to suggest we get another bottle of this very good red," he added. "But a couple of questions first.

"So far as you know, did your mum continue to get part of his pay until the end of hostilities? And do you remember if he was demobilised in the normal way – suit, shirts, raincoat, hat, all the standard demob paraphernalia – when he came home? That could be significant."

"There was never much money coming in, but it had to be coming from somewhere.

"And I do seem to remember a green sports jacket that he hated, and what I think they call a Robin Hood trilby hat with a feather. Both of them lived full-time in the wardrobe. Does that sound typical?"

"Yes, Bernie, very typical. By the way, do you think I might start calling you Bernard? I truly can't get comfortable with 'Bernie'..."

"By all means," I said. (I was the one doing the chuckling now.)

# CHAPTER 15

Shakespeare, if I remember rightly, said that wine heightened the desire but hindered the performance. He was wrong. Or maybe that was just the way it took him.

It didn't do that with me. Rather, it provided an erection that felt almost anaesthetised, but happily fixed in the action-stations mode.

Mel was delighted. At least for the first half hour or so. We decided we'd have to try it again, for experimental purposes, when next we could afford a decent bottle.

She made me so happy. Those amazing, bedroom-blue eyes and the way she dragged me in during her most desperate moments, her hands clasping my bum. Heaven on earth, thunder in heaven. I adored her.

Then, cuddling her, I would get silly.

And we'd both end up.

With the giggles.

Next day was Saturday. We needed to shop. For fun, we loved to mooch around Harrods Food Hall or else Fortnums, but for stocking the larder it had to be one of the price-cutters. Our pockets wouldn't even stretch as far as Waitrose, but it was still nice to shop around. Which was exactly what we were doing that morning, prowling around, enjoying the gorgeous smells in the Food Hall.

Suddenly, a voice I knew very well chilled the air.

"Berneee!" It was Brian's most recent – or perhaps not so recent – ladyfriend, Berenice, the aspiring commedienne who somehow knew everything and everyone. Words dropped anywhere in her vicinity immediately grew wings.

Curiously, it could work in both directions. Berenice seemed always to know whatever it was you wanted to know yourself but somehow usually arrived there before you.

"Berenice, how lovely to see you. And to hear you. The voice is in good order. How are things going for you? Last time I saw you, you were auditioning for – oh, what was it, the female lead in "Arden of Feversham"?

She pulled a face that spoke whole stanzas, blew out her cheeks, and told the world what she thought of it. "Bloody auditions. I've told them, I don't do auditions any more. Not for arty-farty, semi-pro companies who don't deserve me. They *know* what I can do, so I told them what *they* could effing well do! I'm a *comedienne*, not a bloody stand-up comic. *Comedienne*, as in *Comedie Francaise*. Which is not a bloody music hall.

"Anyway, who's this?" She was looking at Mel, apparently admiring her curls.

"I'm Mel," said Mel. "For your information, I'm not 'this', I don't do 'this'. I've never played 'this' and I certainly wouldn't audition for the part."

"Oh, bravo!" said Berenice, genuinely impressed. "I love your hair, by the way."

They both laughed. "Anyway, since you asked, I'm Bernie's bedmate. That's alliteration, of course. Next year, he might even make an honest woman of me, but as I've never been a dishonest woman, I'm in no rush. He's warm and cuddly and makes me happy."

"Who's a lucky boy, then?" Berenice was looking at me. "Look after her or I might just be tempted to steal her from you."

"I'm not sure Mel leans that way."

"I'm not sure either," said Mel. "You'd better give me time to think about it."

"Got time for a coffee?" Berenice smiled.

I'm not quite sure at what point the three of us had become friends, but I knew it had happened. Mel could hold her own with anyone now. She wasn't my shy teen any more.

We ordered coffee and sat down to chat.

"Hey, Bernie, have you heard from Brian?"

I shook my head, not so much to signal no, but because I wasn't sure I'd heard right. "No, I haven't. Have you."

"He's in Berlin. I was talking to him only a couple of nights ago. He's back with Frieda, in case you didn't know. Did you ever meet Frieda?"

I just shook my head. "You know he's got half of Interpol and MI6 looking for him...Or perhaps you didn't? They seem to think he's got himself mixed up in something secret and sinister."

"Well, I don't think he's in hiding or anything. He's just decided he wants to be with Frieda and he's not coming back. Frieda's become a multi-millionairess by the way, winning some lottery or other. So they've probably just swanned off somewhere. Don't ask me where. Transsylvania, I shouldn't be surprised. She's probably bought Dracula's castle!

"Oh, and yes, he gave me a message for you. 'Look after the magazine. The job's yours as far as he's concerned. And don't let Brendan Madders anywhere near it, he'll only fuck it up for you.'

If I looked as stunned as I felt... No, I didn't know how I felt. Nor did I know what to say or not to say about Brian.

A voice, which could have been my yiddishe momma's, was telling me "Stay schtum." At that moment it seemed by far the best of available options.

# CHAPTER 16

"What did you think of Berenice?" Bernie talking. In bed with Mel.

"She's probably an acquired taste. Did you ever acquire a taste for Berenice? Or a taste *of* Berenice?"

"Fifth amendment on that one!"

"So you did?"

"Did what?"

"Have a taste of Berenice."

"Did you ever consider becoming a lawyer?"

"Would I have been a good one?"

"Undoubtedly."

"Cuddle me."

"I thought I was..."

"Tighter."

Cuddling progresses, conversation lapses. Mel gets laid. So does Bernie. Sighs of contentment. Then:

"Do you suppose Berenice is up to something?"

"Always."

"She fancies you..."

"Heaven forfend. I'm not nearly rich enough. Anyway, I'm booked.

"For the season?"

"For life. Unless you've changed your mind...Besides, you heard her. It's you she fancies. She wants to steal you from me."

"Some chance. I'm not really like that."

"You were doing well enough with Aggi..."

"It's different with Aggi. Aggi's a pal. We only really cuddle..."

"Is that what you call it? It looked good to me."

"Perhaps you should join us?"

"Enough, woman." He kisses her on the corner of the mouth. "You might not need beauty sleep but I do..."

"I'll tell you what," Mel says. "I didn't put my diaphragm in."

"Naughty girl." Bernie already sounds three-quarters asleep. "So it's in the lap of the gods then, is it?"

Next morning comes in a flash. And, with it, the unwelcome realisation it's a work day. Coffee, toast, marmalade. Clean teeth again.

Fly out of the flat. Down to the Tube. Just see the train leave. Cuss words. Then another realisation, much more welcome. There's no one to give out a bollocking any more. I'm the editor, albeit an editor with no staff. Ah, well, *Ca ne fait rien*. Or, "San Fairy Ann," as Bernie's gran used to say.

Then I spot Brendan Madders sitting in my chair, sleeves rolled up to his elbows. "Thought I'd give you a hand," he says. "You never really forget the old tricks."

I hide my alarm. Or try to.

"Nice to get up early again. Just like the old days."

Now I'm really getting scared. But I'll soon take the wind out of his sails. I haven't told him the news about Brian yet.

"I'm glad you're here, Brendan. I think you know Berenice Fitzwilliam, don't you?"

His face lit up. I was sure he knew her "in the Biblical sense" as some folk would delicately put it. "Indeed I do," he confirmed. "We've been friends for, well, longer than perhaps I should say since we're talking about a lady."

"Mel and I met her in Harrods Food Hall only yesterday. Brendan, she'd had a telephone call only the evening before, from someone we both know."

He looked at me inquiringly.

"She'd been speaking with Brian."

"Good God! Did she say where he was?"

"More to the point, he didn't say where he was. And she hadn't realised he was missing. You'll love this. As we first suspected, he is back with Frieda. But where they are now, the two of them, is anybody's guess. Don't laugh, she's won a king's bloody ransome – as Berenice puts it – in one of these European lotteries and the pair of them have just vanished. So god knows where they are. Berenice reckons somewhere in Transsylvania, but then she always did have a quaint sense of humour."

"Unless, of course, the idea is to lay a false scent." Trust Brendan, he being a hunting man. "Think about it. I've known Berenice for years. She'd think nothing of telling a whopper if it was to help Brian out of a spot."

"I'd say, Bernard, the only positive thing that does come out of it is that Brian is alive."

"But, for whatever reason, doesn't want to be found," I added. "All of which puts us back just about where we started. Thanks, Berenice."

"Don't be unkind, Bernard. She has a good heart and I'm sure she meant well."

"You would say that, Brendan. You've been in her knickers. You owe her a debt."

He had the grace to look guilty for a moment. Just a little bit. "We do go back rather a long way," he offered, as if by way of amelioration. "I suppose she does come across as a trifle coarse these days..."

"No she doesn't, Brendan," I reassured him. "She just comes across as an actress - an actress who's been around the block a few times. She's all right. She did actually make a pass at Mel, but Mel handled it perfectly. Anyway, since you're here, Brendan, I don't suppose you feel like knocking out a few film reviews, do you? I'm sure you can still thread up the old Bell & Howell..."

"Don't mind if I do," he said, affecting an appalling Cockney accent.

"Not bad," I said, "for a gent who's never been further east than Fenchurch Street station. My dear mum, let me tell you, was born in Exeter Street, E1, just off the Mile End Road, which is well within tolling distance of Bow Bells. She could have been a Pearly Queen by now."

Brendan turned towards me as he was halfway through the door. "Oh, Bernard, while I think of it, I may have some information that could throw some light on your father's RAF record. It's probably best if we meet up again when we've more time. I've got films to watch."

# CHAPTER 17

The more I thought about it, the less convinced I was by Berenice's account of Brian's "doings" with Frieda. It would be a relief to think he was still with us on planet Earth as distinct from in the earth, but somehow the tale just didn't hold water. Apart from anything else, the Brian I knew was infuriatingly logical – to the point of pedantry at times – and, in my experience, utterly reliable.

He just didn't do the things Berenice had described. On the other hand, as one of my small voices was pointing out, he'd married three times, been divorced twice, in both instances on the grounds of multiple infidelities. Did that make him the same Mr. Reliable I'd just been claiming for him?

As for Frieda – although I'd never met the woman, she didn't sound the steady type, did she? (That was me asking myself, by the way.) But if not steady, was she not even more likely to be fascinating? I started pondering on the allure she might have for Brian. And then I had another thought. Although Brian was shamelessly attracted to pretty women – the young Jewish journalist had been an exquisite little slip of a thing – he could have been lured by a quite different characteristic. Politics.

The politics of the Left, of course. Here was a whole new can of worms. Politically, Brian and I were aligned closely enough to make precious little difference, with the exception, that is, of physical attraction.

Although Brian could be sorely tempted by a pretty face, a striking figure, there was one characteristic that drew him like the proverbial moth to a candle. He could not resist a woman who burned with socialist fervour. She could be skinny, almost without tits at all, big nose, thin lips, poor complexion, dreary hair, mole on her chin. It wouldn't matter a damn. Socialist fervour would overcome all these shortcomings. It fired his loins. He'd be a man possessed.

As for the physically unfavoured female, she'd find herself being possessed like never before in her life. And it wouldn't surprise me if he actually liked BO. I could think of stranger fetishes, couldn't you, Dr Krafft Ebing?

If this Frieda were one of those totally committed women, would she even dream of buying such thing as a lottery ticket, if it came to that? And if she did – and just say it won – what would she do? Give the proceeds to the Party, presumably. If the Party would accept the gift, that is.

There were an awful lot of ifs in this scenario.

But, perish the thought, I could imagine Brian stoking the furnace of some modern-day Rosa Luxemburg, all political fire and vaginal self-destruction; but I had to admit, it was all getting rather fanciful.

And in the meantime, I had "Frame" to put to bed. There was also a documentary film festival coming up in Brighton the following month. Maybe Mel could get some time off and come with me.

Mel, in the meantime, had had a call at work from Berenice. I didn't realise they'd swapped numbers but I supposed they must have done. Apparently, she'd relented about doing auditions, because she had nailed the female lead in "Arden of Feversham" which is, as I gathered, an important play, pre-dating Shakespeare and heralding all kinds of innovations. With Berenice in the leading role, there might well be a few more on the way, a little voice kept telling me. Heaven knows, I shouldn't have wanted to be directing her.

She was rather hoping, she said, that Mel would spend some time helping her learn her lines. Surprisingly, Mel was quite neutral about it. She'd never done anything like that before, she said, but she didn't mind "giving it a go".

"Watch yourself with Berenice," I laughed.

"Are you worried?" (Mel laughing back.) "What's the worst she can do, get me tiddly and seduce me?"

"Are you hoping?"

"No." It wasn't what I'd call a foot-down no"; more of a "maybe" no. The kind of no that has a little bend in the middle. Very much a girl's no, in fact. One that always leaves you feeling you're in with a chance.

"You still want to marry me?"

"Silly bugger," she said. "I certainly wouldn't want to live with Berenice."

"That's good then. When will you be going?"

"Not arranged yet. She'll come and pick me up."

I blew her a kiss, just a prelude to pulling her in for a proper buss. "I love you," I told her. "I don't mind what you get up to, so long as you don't change sides on me..."

"As if." That was a complete sentence. She tightened her arms around my neck. "She hasn't got one like yours." Her giggling was now tickling my ear. "At least, I don't think so."

"Hmm, okay. But watch out if she wants to show you her toys. And especially look out for cucumbers and big carrots. D'you know what they used to call those big carrots? Widow comforters!"

No answer, just a (fairly) gentle punch.

"Come to bed?" I whispered.

"We haven't had dinner."

"Plenty of time for dinner. What is it, anyway?"

"Your turn is what it is. I did last night."

"Come and see what we've got..."

"What about bed?"

"Plenty of time for bed."

# CHAPTER 18

I've begun to feel just a shade guilty about the number of times Brendan picks up the bill for our shared lunches and occasional dinners. I console myself, however, with the thought of how undoubtedly loaded he is and his confession of how costly he is to feed. Add to that, how costly to clothe; sometimes I suspect even his underpants are tailor-made in Savile Row. Personally, I'd be terrified even to fart in them.

Nevertheless, here we were again, this time in his club (or should I say Club?), which he has foresworn me not to name. Strange name really, which starts off sounding Greek and concludes with a Latin suffix. There's private education and scholarship for you.

But let's not poke too much fun at Brendan Madders. At least it isn't pretension. Whatever you may be tempted to think of him, he is definitely for real. A real gent? Maybe not. But definitely real.

Bit of an epicure, too. Doesn't believe in serious talk while you're indulging the love of fine food. Which leads us (or, rather, leads him) into a discussion of the term gourmand. He assures me, pausing briefly from mastication, the true meaning relates to appreciation of the culinary arts and definitely not to the deadly sin of gluttony. I suggest to him that, sin or not, gluttony can be seriously deadly on its own terms.

Patience is duly rewarded, however, when coffee and cognac signal the time to talk treason.

"Your daddy..." he says, sounding just a weeny bit befuddled already and leading me to wonder if he'd indulged one or two pre-prandial Courvoisiers before I turned up.

I stop him right away. "My daddy he never was," I insist, "except in the technical sense. The only time I called him that, when I was about three and he was just home from the war, he told me in no uncertain terms I was never, ever to call him daddy. Never, ever again. Looking back, it felt rather like hate at first sight."

"Shall we call him your father, then? Can you stand that?"

I managed to combine a nod with a half-smile.

"About your father, then, specifics are thin on the ground, as you yourself seem to have discovered. As far as concerns the RAF, they don't seem to exist. There may be good reasons for that but let that go for now.

"What I have been able to unearth may nevertheless (hiccup) be relevant to his case by virtue of certain persuasive similarities..." (Signal to waiter for more cognac.)

"First of all, you have to cast your mind back to the early 1940s. There was a war going on. With Germany. And it wasn't going awfully well for our side. Rommel was still ruling the roost in the Western desert. No Monty yet. No hitting the enemy for six. Our tanks were worse than bloody useless. Might as well have gone into battle in Morris Minors. The only way we could hit back was from the air.

"We knew that, of course..."

"As one would," I concurred.

"...which is why Egypt was dotted here, there and everywhere, with RAF bases. Mostly they were operating Wellington bombers, Beauforts, Mosquitos. I flew in Wimpeys, by the way. Nothing to do with George Wimpey, the builders, in case you're wondering...it was the nickname they gave the Wellington bomber. God knows why.

"Well, they were doing a good job, making life as hellish as they could for Rommel and his Afrika Corps. Are you with me still?"

The truth was, I didn't know whether to laugh or cry. But I was trying not to show it. Meanwhile, across the table from me, the Air Commodore was refuelling with aviation-grade cognac.

"That many aircraft took a lot of keeping in the air," he continued. "A lot of pilots – one for each aeroplane, of course, plus a few spares – and any number of armourers, engineers and mechanics, communications specialists, you name it."

I could see what he meant. He was having difficulty enough getting his tongue around "communications specialists" as it was. Try saying "specialists" when you've had a few.

"The thing to remember was, they weren't just 'airmen'. Every one of them had had to be trained to the nth degree. You couldn't turn a butcher's boy into an armourer overnight. It took time, and there was never enough of that.

"Trained specialists – especially communications types – were like gold dust. Men who could go into the innards of a wireless installation, test it, take it apart, put it back together again... well, they didn't grow on date palms down at the oasis.

"They were as crucial as pilots and took a damned sight longer to train.

"Men like your father were press-ganged out of the merchant navy to serve as wireless technicians in the RAF. And that, dear boy, tells us how your father came to be in Egypt instead of sunbathing on the Copacabana while the refridge...the refridgeration ships were loading up with beef in Fray Bentos or wherever."

It didn't seem worth pointing out that the Copacabana was in Brazil, not the Argentine. He was far too well away to know the difference. I just let him have his head.

"So far, dear boy, all this is based on fact. Recorded fact. But now we come to what you might call 'enlightened supposition'.

"No inside information or privileged access. Just the recollections of one or two reliable sources who were there at the time. It's all we have to work with."

! won't say I was hopeful exactly, but if there were to be anything revealing, this was where it just might begin.

"Please carry on, Brendan," I said. "As my mother used to say, I'm all ears."

"All right. Let's suppose you're a commanding officer. You're busting a gut to keep your unit airborne and functional in spite of casualties, aircraft losses, equipment failures, you name it. And you're still only just keeping your head above water.

"You now discover you've got another kind of problem. Let's say you've got a hot-tempered airman who's always getting into fights.

"Or suppose you've got an airman who's an unreconstructed homosexual. Apart from anything else, it's strictly against King's Regulations. Instant dismissal from the ranks.

"Now think again. You're in the middle of a fucking desert, you've got Jerry trying to wipe you out and this gay airman happens to be the only top-notch Marconi-trained communications technician for miles around.

"What do you do?

"I'll tell you what an old chum of mine did.

"This wireless wallah's been caught in the act with another airman. A younger man at that. My chum is well aware that if he put in for another communications tech, god only knew how long he'd have to wait or what kind of replacement he'd get.

"So I'll tell you what he did. He kept him on. Warned him with instant drowning in the nearest wadi if he ever let his dick out of his trousers for anything except to piss.

But kept him on. Because as far as my chum was concerned, nothing, absolutely nothing, was going to take precedence over keeping his squadron airborne and operational. Not a fucking thing.

"He knew what a chance he was taking. But with so much going on, so many conflicting priorities, he reckoned he'd probably get away with it.

"And he did exactly that."

Taking everything into consideration, cognac included, it had been a virtuoso performance, but it wasn't over yet. I'd occasionally heard of people drinking themselves sober, but this was the first time I could recall witnessing it. Brendan actually seemed more in control than he'd been at the beginning. He focused on me again.

"I'm not saying this is what happened with your father, Bernard, but it is the kind of thing that could have happened.

"Then, in the total confusion of the Middle East campaign - the bombings, the strafings, the fire-fighting - his details disappear along with so much else. In the chaos, he stops being an individual and becomes a kind of lost soul: almost a non-Airman in a theatrical uniform.

"Is this making any sense, Bernard?"

"A little more now," I tell him, "but I'm still not sure. It all seems so... far fetched. But then I've never been in a war."

Then chance catches everyone out by delivering a curve ball. Our non-Airman, possibly my father, catches typhoid fever, gets transferred to an American military hospital and eventually recovers just in time to be sent home by hospital ship.

"And all this time, your mum has still been receiving his pay, or whatever part of it she's been getting, because everybody's too damned busy to unravel the mess.

"Finally, back in Whitehall, some baffled clerk decides the best thing to do is wipe the records clean, so this non-Airman, who may or may not be your father, ceases to exist completely. He is repatriated back to the UK, now all in hospital blue, and when hostilities have ceased he gets his demob suit with all the rest.

"And, if you think that sounds complicated, you should just have been there."

"But Brendan," I ask him, shaking my head, "what about his identity discs, his dog tags? He must have been wearing them ...mustn't he?"

Brendan looks more pensive than he has at any time.

"You do seem to have a point there," he concedes. Then he brightens. "I didn't say it was all gospel, did I? I just thought you deserved an informed overview."

Informed overview? It seemed to me more as though he'd made up the whole bloody thing.

Then, catching my eye, he looked uncharacteristically sad.

"Fortune of war, old lad... Misfortune of war? It touches all of us, you know."

Even my father? The jury would stay out on that one for a long, long time.

# CHAPTER 19

It was time Mel and I were married. We'd done all the talking. Jumped the gun by a country mile (just a saying I rather like) and my wonderful sweetheart had started looking dewy-eyed at other people's babies. Broodiness couldn't be far behind. And as the appointed editor of "Frame", name on the masthead, I was making enough – is it ever enough? – for a tiny family to get by. Getting Mel pregnant was the easiest thing in the world. And by far the most enjoyable.

We'd often talked about why we were so much in love. Apart from the obvious physical attraction, there was something else that we shared. We both cared about each other every bit as much as we cared for each other. I'd never felt so secure as I felt now, embraced by her love; at least not since my baby days when mum was my everything. (From that, draw any conclusion you wish, but you will probably be wrong.)

I knew Mel felt the same, not just from what she said but from the way, and the warmth, with which she clung to me. It needed no interpreter; I was getting broody too.

We named the day. We told our friends. And, yes, we told both families. Don't ask me how, but both sides behaved impeccably. It was possibly that, even more than the wedding itself, that had me walking around in a daze.

My mother was kissing everybody, especially Mel and me. My father even smiled and clasped my shoulder, as well as giving Mel a squeeze and a peck on the cheek. My Aunt Jazz, as usual, talked the hind leg off a donkey, fortunately without revealing any serious family secrets. Mel's mum and dad just looked happy – well, I'd made an honest woman of their daughter, hadn't I? And about time too, as they saw it.

All our work friends were good mixers by nature, especially Aggs, who was kissing anyone who looked in the least bit receptive, male or female. She planted a whopper on me, accompanied by a knowing smile. A goodbye kiss if ever there was one.

Mel's uncles, the two Royal Navy petty officers, had discovered the main beer supply. It was in the kitchen, where they hung out till the ale ran out and they flaked out. Or sneaked out to the pub – it hardly mattered which.

It was altogether a happier, more peaceful day than we could possibly have hoped for. We cut the wedding cake, posed for photographs (except for the uncles in the kitchen) and, quite suddenly as it seemed, it was time for Mel and me to beat a timely retreat.

We'd decided, for fun, to base our honeymoon on the classic dirty-weekend. Gainsborough Pictures would have been proud of us. Brighton on the train, seafront hotel, room with sea view. We didn't sign in as Mr and Mrs Smith because we didn't need to. Wonders would never cease.

There was no chance of concealing our newly-wed status, however. Confetti fell everywhere as we walked and when we came to unpack.

Dinner was nothing special but we didn't give a damn. We'd been eating each other, one way or another, for half the night. (Only half the night? Remember, we'd been jumping the gun for over two years.)

And that luxury, tropical honeymoon that most newly-wed couples can only dream of...well, it was going to have to remain a dream for us, too, at least for the time being.

# CHAPTER 20

I was determined to play fair with Mel. At the moment, the future for us wore nappies. All we had to do was make it happen.

We knew that would be fun. Less fun would be finding somewhere else to live. Our tiny pied a terre, which is all it really was, was just big enough for two, not two plus baby and everything else that went with her or him.

That wasn't the only thing on my mind, however. If I were going to be a father, I would have to be a very different one from my own father. Sounds simple? Yes, doesn't it? Not for the man in my shoes, it wasn't. I didn't know how to do it. I'd never had the experience. I didn't really know how to be a good father. It began to prey on my mind, not least because of something even more troubling.

Hadn't my father been in much the same boat? And on a much bigger, war-torn sea?

Was I about to begin a guilt trip concerning dad?

I put it out of my head, which seemed a good thing at the time. Wasn't it easier, much easier, to leave the pieces where they'd fallen?

The simple truth was I'd rather have walked in front of a bus than become a father like he'd been for me. But was the simple truth the only truth? Or was the simple truth oversimplified?

Naturally, I talked it through with Mel who, in this respect, was very much old-school. It was still early days. We hadn't stopped using contraception yet. There was plenty of time, and she was happy enough to think it would all come right naturally. All prospective fathers were bags of nerves. She was sure I'd make a lovely dad.

Of course, that was what I wanted too. And I knew, no doubts at all, that she would be a wonderful, loving mum. But could I possibly live up to her expectations? And was the newly discovered guilt trip going to haunt me, possibly big-time?

Yet here we were, married and wanting to start a family.

I knew deep down that I could never become a wife-beater. I wouldn't harm a hair of Mel's precious head. But would I possess the same composure, faced with a squalling, red-faced baby who, through no fault of her or his own, couldn't yet respond to reason?

God, why did life have to be so difficult? (He wasn't telling.)

Then there was money. The two of us had always managed just about on our combined earnings, but babies cost plenty and there was no allowance for first children. Much as I loved "Frame", I now needed a job that paid more.

Headaches, headaches. Admittedly, not all of my fears were entirely rational.

But some were.

I'd made light of my confession to Mel, my "scoutmaster confession". Was it really a confession at all? Had I failed to make a properly clean breast of things simply because Mel had made owning-up so easy for me? Or was it because I was so afraid she might not if I told everything?

Still no answer from the Man Upstairs, but the other voice, the little, inner voice, was never shy. "Why rock the boat? Aren't things good? So why be hard on yourself? Bury it."

But burials in the recesses of your brain are never peaceful, as any psychotherapist will tell you.

Common sense, that other little voice, warned I was storing up trouble; but when had I ever listened to common sense?

And was I truly sure that my, shall we say, off-beat sexual tastes were as safely consigned to the past as I liked to think they were?

I won't say I lived in fear, but fear knew where I lived.

# CHAPTER 21

There were simple answers, of course. Simple for me, at any rate. My young and cheerfully supportive GP introduced me to an olive green friend called Librium. Even the colour was restful and inspired a reassuring degree of confidence. Pop one, I soon discovered, and in very little time I was able to cope with problems that would otherwise have taken away my placidity.

Even now I don't blame him for anything, simply because in my view there was nothing to blame him for. The olive green babies engineered a character change in me. I didn't worry about problems at work, just reviewed them and overcame them. Confidence flowed in my blood stream. I chatted to managers and directors in my new workplace, addressed them by their first names, and they liked my progressive, easy-going style.

They even liked my work and rewarded me with regular pay rises.

Mel and I were having fun. We went out with friends to clubs and parties. I even became a passable dancer – no, not ballroom – when previously I couldn't be persuaded to get up and dance at all. Now, especially at parties, I couldn't wait to start or bear to finish.

We then produced two bonny sons in two years and I adored them both. I was a proud dad, a loving husband and happy with myself.

Then, something rather awful happened. HM Government, in its infinite crass stupidity, decided that Librium, my precious olive green babies, were bad for us. Dangerous was the word they used, as I recall. I felt that the Government should be looking closer to home. My GP agreed. But that was that.

Life without Librium began. The politicos didn't have the same reserves about Valium at that time, but all that did was make me sleep. Rather like bloody politicians, actually. They were – the tablets, not the politicos – supposedly similar to Librium according to my shame-faced GP, but neither of us truly believed that. Very much second best as usual. Best, in fact, didn't even come into it.

Clang! That was my confidence, my self-esteem, my joie de vivre and much else hitting the concrete floor. It all went to hell. I didn't hit Mel or the boys, but I just wasn't the loving husband and dad any more.

After besieging my GP for months, he put me on anti-depressants – a whole string of different names over a period, until we found something that worked after a fashion. And that, as they say, dear reader, is where I've been ever since. We all have our cross, don't we?

But the Librium years had been good. Not perfect, of course. I always had the slight worry that Brian would just reappear one day and demand his old job back. It didn't happen. Or, for a little while, that Jerry would turn up and demand that I turned my old movie treatment into a shooting script. He didn't. And I rather think he eventually got the sack.

Unusual, I'd been led to believe, in an oil company. You had to be a very bad boy for that to happen, another old oil man had once told me.

"What ever happened with Berenice?" I wondered aloud, one evening while were quietly skipping through the days' papers. Mel had recently taken to wearing reading glasses. "Did she ever get her part in 'Arden of Feversham'?"

"Probably."

"Did you ever help her...?"

"Help her?"

"Learn her part?"

"Oh, yes..."

"We never did go to see it, did we?" I prompted.

"No, I don't think we did. Can't think why..."

I responded with a little non-committal "Mmm," as much inquiry as comment.

"You're fishing," said Mel. "Why would you do that?" It was one of her cleverest sallies. She was very good at them; never pointed, never in the least bit argumentative, just gently inquiring. It always made me laugh. Much better to laugh, and love her, than to argue.

I couldn't say "No reason" because I did have a reason. "Just curious," I said, which was almost as banale.

"I know what you're curious about," she looked at me over her reading specs. "Are you going to be honest and ask me?"

"Oh, Mel, you're wonderful," I told her.

"Berenice told me much the same thing."

"Did she now? Had you been...especially wonderful?"

"You'd have to ask Berenice..."

"Would you like me to?"

"I'd love you to..."

"Shall we come to bed?"

"Bernie," she said, after we'd sated each other and got our breath back, "have you been reading Noel Coward again?"

"My favourite writer..."

"I know. I sometimes think I live with him."

"Sollocks," I said to her.

"Oh, come on," she turned her head to look at me. "It's not a sollocks moment. It's a Mel and Bernie moment. Isn't it?"

We kissed. And slept like kittens.

# CHAPTER 22

"Did you hear what happened to Jerry?" Brendan Madders's voice sounded a little husky over the phone. "He got the sack apparently. Very sad. I liked him"

"Hard not to like Jerry," I said. "But he was very good at getting out of line. He never quite caught on to how things had changed since Dudley's time. RusPet were never going to be another BP. He'd always fancied Dudley's job, by the way. Not a chance, of course. Jerry had – still has, I suppose – the gift of the gab, but not the gravity, not the background."

"The rumour is that there were some irregularities in the entertainment budget among other things," Madders picked up. "But then you'd probably know all about that. And didn't he make a pass at Mel?"

"Well, sort of," I half corrected him. "Mel thought it was funny. He didn't, as you might imagine. I wasn't laughing my socks off either.

"But speaking of entertaining, Brendan, did he never take you on the unofficial Leopold Bloom pub crawl? All the naughtiest barmaids, all the crustiest bars, all the juiciest tarts, including the ones giving sneak previews; the cabmen's shelter if it's still standing, and a visit to Cunty Kate's parlour. Or what passes for it these days.

"Strictly unofficial, as I say, and always on the move. Like the mobile crap game in that story of Damon Runyon's.

"A night to remember, especially if you ended up with a dose of clap, care of Cunty Kate's. There were no guarantees. Remember what Kate used to tell them. 'Stop that and start worse...'"

"Such reminiscences, dear boy. You make me feel quite deprived. Where would we be without the likes of Jerry?"

"Never mind the likes of Jerry, what about the likes of Brian? And where he might be?"

"Wish I could bring you up to speed," Madders said sadly. "You know, I still think he's going to turn up one day."

"Unless he's dead. Or wants somebody to think he is."

Madders was always a great yarn spinner. Aren't all writers? If we weren't, we'd all be court reporters. "What's the latest on Berenice, by the way?" I asked him, not entirely without ulterior motive.

"Oh, Berenice? Don't ask. We've been friends for a long time, she and I. But if you ask me, I'd say she's swung the other way good and proper..."

"You mean good and improper, don't you?"

"Oh – oh, yes. I see what you mean. Good and improper." Then, as though correcting himself, "Good and proper for her though, I expect. Not to mention well considered. A fair few lesbian producers and directors these days."

"I think it was always so, Brendan. You just didn't spot them. Actresses, too. Let's be honest, acting's always been a pretty gay profession. More or less expected with the boys."

"Do you really think so?" he ventured. It felt like he was venturing.

"How could it be otherwise?" I suggested. "You sound surprised. And you a public schoolboy?"

I relayed this conversation to Mel that evening as we drove over to Berenice's flat. Once you'd got accustomed to Berenice and her ways – I nearly said "little ways", but that would have been underselling – her ways were neither little nor particularly eccentric. The ways were as much a part of Berenice as her face or the way she had of sitting in an easy chair.

Not many people liked her from the very first. She became comfortable with use, if that isn't a vulgar way of putting it, and after a while she was... just Berenice. Occasionally vulgar, always to the point, shameless about herself – unashamed is probably a better word – and honest to your face. All in all, I'd come to find her refreshing. Mel, I think, was rather fond of her, though it had taken a little time and work.

As we sat gossiping, swapping news and updating each other about our not-so-mundane lives, it felt strange to think that, in a short while, the three of us were almost certainly going to be rolling together - "bullock naked" as my gorgeous betrothed put it - in Berenice's rather extraordinary bed, which could have been designed for this express purpose and quite possibly was.

We shared our warmth, our scents, our unique and individual skin-feels and tastes, our urges to cling, everything that made us "us". And then the sharings and exchanges born in the mind reach out to the limbs and the body. Beauty isn't just in the eye of the beholder and desire certainly isn't.

Love and lust are for sharing. And so is a super king-size bed.

"Watch," says Berenice. As she rotates herself momentarily from Mel's side, I see that she is now wearing a black thong that holds in place a most realistic and fully erect penis, also black, which - unlike my own - will neither wilt nor tire.

With adept fingers, she separates the petals of Mel's vagina and nudges the tip of the penis against the delicate opening now revealed. She then eases the entire piece into the waiting cavity in a single, confident move, performed with the consummate ease and grace that come only with assiduous practice.

Both women respond with deft movements and evident pleasure. Evidently, too, not for the first time. When they come to a climax, it's so perfectly orchestrated: they might equally have been synchronised swimmers. Then, having kissed, whispered and kissed again, they begin to undulate anew.

I'm lost in admiration. Such a perfectly rehearsed routine.

Men, I conclude, are by nature lazy. Why burn energy when you can just watch the girls? Such elegant movers. So good at what they do.

Why hadn't god made me a lesbian? (No knitting jokes please.

# CHAPTER 23

The fun and games are over for the evening. We've backtracked and established it's Cordelia, not Cunnilingus, who is Lear's favourite daughter and all three of us are affected by that sense of ease which comes about only when the urgent need for sex has been satisfied.

It's when satisfied souls – and bodies, of course – feel like talking. The need for stimulation is replaced by the need to ramble.

"Do you think we're playing a dangerous game?" Berenice speaks, apparently to no one in particular. The unexpected words float like smoke in the room. She seems in no hurry for an answer. Perhaps she realises it isn't an easy question. Of course, she does.

As so often, I embark on an answer without quite knowing where it might end up. "Are you wondering if the game is dangerous in itself? Or is the game dangerous because it's us playing it?"

A short spell of silence follows. It probably feels like much longer than it is.

"Okay, then," I continue. "A slightly different question. Are we dangerous? I don't think I am. I try to be careful not to let my tongue run away with me..."

"It can run away with me any time," Berenice smiles. "Your audition was impressive. Make sure you leave your number."

"I think you'll find he's under contract to me," says Mel, looking a little like the cat who got the cream - though I suspect her claws may have been out all the same.

"Couldn't we come to some arrangement?" Berenice smiles again. "Do you have an agent?"

"Bernie's my agent."

Bernie plumps for a diversionary action. "Did I see some cold roast chicken and chilled white burgundy in the kitchen? Just a suggestion..."

"You did, darling," says Berenice. "You wouldn't care to bring it in, would you?"

"Chicken and dry white sounds perfect but go easy with the 'darlings.'" This, from Mel, could be described as a deceptive ping-pong shot across the bows.

"Don't panic, my sweet," Berenice to Mel. "Stage 'darlings' don't count..."

"How does one tell the difference?"

"Do you really not know?" Berenice kisses Mel on the lips with more than a hint of intent. "Does that make it any clearer?"

"It makes something clearer."

"Yesss? And what's that, pray?" Distinctly Shakespearian.

"You do rather fancy me, don't you? It's not just a game?"

"Ooh, where's the difference? The game itself is real, don't you find?"

"I'm still making my mind up. Kiss me again."

"Let me convince you."

It's a kiss that deepens, makes its case abundantly clear. There's the possibility of commitment on both sides. "Are you happy, my dear?"

"Happy? Yes. Everyone needs to be loved."

"Bernie," Mel beckons me with a slight lift and turn of her head. When I come close, both women pull me into a triple embrace. We all kiss fervently. It feels like we are sealing something that isn't exactly sacred, could just be disastrous, but which the three of us have agreed to embark upon.

"Shall we share the wedding breakfast? All three of us?" Berenice claps her hands like a young girl.

\*\*\*\*\*\*\*\*\*\*\*\*\*\*\*\*\*\*\*\*\*\*\*\*\*\*\*\*

Chicken slices. Crusty French bread. Fresh butter. Crisp, cold white burgundy. Lips still slightly bruised. Bodies and limbs still experiencing a tangible after-flutter of desire.

"I'm not sure we ought to drive home tonight," says Mel. "I feel quite fluttery."

"You too?" says Berenice, whose ears are as sharp as any cat's. She and Mel both look at me.

"Beds are also for sleeping in." I am looking directly at Berenice's magnificent divan, as wide as the steppes of Central Asia.

"What were you saying?" said Mel. "I'm sure you said something about the Steppes of Central Asia."

"Yes, I think I did." Then, shaking my head, "Don't ask."

I wanted nothing more than to hold her closely in my arms again. And, with her, sleep.

# CHAPTER 24

Next morning, driving home. Mel at the wheel. Neither of us showing any apparent remorse about the games we'd been playing the night before.

"Have you enjoyed yourself?"

"Uh-hu," Mel nods in agreement but wisely concentrates on keeping us safe on the M25. Reluctantly, I have to concede she is now a better driver than I am. Since her last promotion, she has had a company car and does more miles than I do. And faster.

While she deals with the traffic, I start playing around in my mind with the catchy little phrase "Stay alive on the M25", easy to remember and easy to sing. Not exactly politically correct, though.

When we come off the orbital motorway, Mel visibly relaxes. "Do you not feel, sometimes, that enjoyment can be a double-edged sword? Like last night. Of course I enjoyed it, who wouldn't? But it's like a drug, isn't it? The more you have, the more you want. Like the old soaks on Gin Lane. You know the picture, the drunken mother more interested in hanging on to her bottle than holding on to her baby?"

"You think you could become addicted?" I ask her. It was the gentlest of challenges.

"I was thinking of you, actually."

"Oh, thank you."

"I'm just being honest."

"That's a double-edged sword as well. Or don't you think so?"

"All I'm saying is" – a classic Mel opening, this: knight to king's bishop three – "all I'm saying is, it cuts both ways... Anyway, I don't want to squabble."

"Neither do I."

"Shall we both shut up then?"

The shut-up holds for about as long as a Middle East ceasefire.

Then, "Can I say something?" says Mel.

"I thought we – "

"We'll need to pick up something for dinner."

"I love you."

"Waitrose first! Show me how much when we get home."

\*\*\*\*\*\*\*\*\*\*\*\*\*\*\*\*\*\*

We emerge from Waitrose with the essentials of a ping-cuisine supper and a dry-ish Italian white that blends in very peaceably without being bland. In minutes we're home.

"Now, what were you going to show me?"

"I need to whisper in your shell-like..."

"That tickles. And it's not a whisper, it's your tongue..."

"Complaining?"

"No. Come to bed."

Mel leads me by the hand, as she has done so many times. As so often, it's she who takes the initiative, shows the way... and I am happy to let her. It tells me something about myself that I'd be loath to reveal even to her. If she should need explanation – which I sincerely doubt. Somewhere deep down I'm still the little boy who slipped into bed with his mum.

And I'm neither proud nor ashamed.

Just happy.

For such a small creature, my Mel has beautifully rounded breasts. What the Germans would call "saftig". Look it up by all means, but I'll tell you, there is no satisfactory English equivalent. Only the Germans truly know what they mean by it. Only the Germans. And me.

Are they the breasts I have desired ever since my young and busty mum told me enough was enough? (As it never was.) Undefined sexual pleasure. Innocent. But sexual nonetheless.

Was this the root cause of my father's insane desire to beat out my infant brains? Families tell stories. I know that he himself had felt desperately deprived, having been breast-fed until at least three, when the jolly milkmaid – his busty mum – had told him there was no more to be had.

Then, when he'd come home from the war and found me happily suckling at my mum's milky nipples, had this been too much for him to bear? Were those magnificent breasts the cause of the war to end all wars between father and son?

If so, how very sad for both of us. If so, a terrible crime with two victims and no perpetrator. In fact, not two but three victims. My poor and so mistreated mum could hardly be blamed for the beauty and bounty of her fulsome boobs.

And here, now, was I. Suckling the breasts, the hardened nipples, of my own beautiful wife. My gloriously endowed Mel. No sin, no guilt or sin, just the natural expression of love, the blissful love of a husband for his bountiful and fecund young wife.

I knew how she longed for a baby. She knew how I longed to make one with her. But perhaps not quite yet? I wasn't sure, but I knew she was the one to persuade me.

# CHAPTER 25

As a couple, we were doing okay. Admittedly, our income wasn't great, but then neither were our debts. On the other hand a pregnancy - not to mention child care - would make a sizeable hole. And it wasn't as if we had a handy mum-in-law just waiting to step into the breach.

Meanwhile Mel had heard about some young mums' groups starting up, where working mums would contribute to running costs while the other mums would provide the childcare. The original suggestion had come from a Finnish girl called Helva who'd experienced similar schemes in her homeland and was keen to look at something like it here.

She and her partner had been asking about the legal aspects and were now keen to test the market. Mel, for one, was in love with the idea. She and Helva, I'd begun to think, were just a bit in love with each other. They fell now into a big, giggling hug.

In Finland, Helva told us - with a slightly disapproving pout - people were more inclined to think communally and liked helping each other. No one was getting rich at it, but they were getting by on it. They had a rota, everyone did their share and the kids were safe and happy. It was the perfect self-help group. It was socialism at ground roots level: very Scandinavian.

"A mums' commune!" said Mel, savouring the very words. It was pure Mel. She was keen to see for herself and was determinedly enthusing the others.

If they were serious, Helva said, she could organise a group visit - "at special-interest group rates," she added. I could sense she and Mel practically packing their bags. You could never mistake when Mel and a friend were hitting it off. From giggles and hugs it rapidly progressed to a supper invitation, trips together, even joint holidays. I didn't need much persuasion.

Helva and her partner, Havel, came around for a meal a few nights later. They made an easy, likeable couple, both in their late twenties and speaking fluent English with that gentle, Scand inflexion that's so easy on the ear, it practically becomes catching.

By the time we got around to tarte citrine and a Finnish liqueur I'd never seen before, it felt like we'd known each other for years.

"Well, Bernie," Havel said to me, leaning back and grinning, "what do you think? Should we let these two women off the leash in Finland for a week? Who knows what they might be up to?"

"You know, I think I might have an idea..."

"Yeah," growled Havel, swinging his head from them to me. "Me also."

It might as well have been decided there and then. Instead, then and there it was decided.

\*\*\*\*\*\*\*\*\*\*\*\*\*\*\*\*\*\*\*\*\*\*\*

When Mel and Helva got back from Helsinki there was no standing in their way. The mums' commune had already been created in their two converging brains and they were full of the excitement that comes of creating something desired, required, needing mostly their enthusiasm and determination. Of these, there was plenty of both.

Just to look at them working, planning, coaxing, persuading, being negotiators, being unstoppable, a force for good, a benevolent whirlwind: it was like nothing I'd witnessed before, a real-life film speeded up. What was making it special, making it happen, was love; loving what they were planning and, clearly, loving each other more than a little, too.

They now trusted each other, depended on each other, they were winning. It was beautiful to see.

Just as important, I felt part of it. They made me happy. I felt nothing but joy and admiration. Nothing could be further from our own rather tawdry midnight games with Berenice. If they loved each other, Helva and Mel – and, just by watching, it was obvious they did – it was a cause for delight and something to share

Our lives had expanded, taken on more meaning. No one had preached to us. It had just happened. We needed each other. We had each other. We all felt it, all wanted it, including Havel. We stayed loose. The secret was staying loose.

But suppose it was just another dangerous game? If that were the case, I wasn't sure I could stand it. In fact, I was sure I couldn't. But, then, it nearly became no game at all.

Mel came home from a get-together looking worse than glum. She perched her bum on the edge of the sofa and I could see right away she wasn't far from tears.

I perched alongside her, put my arm around her shoulders, kissed and squeezed her. "What's happened, sweetheart?" I asked her, gently turning her face towards me.

"Everything. Bloody everything," she said. "It's all going wrong. There's so many things we don't seem to have thought of..."

"Like what?"

She blew out her cheeks and exhaled through pursed lips.

"Like rent money," she spouted, "Like premises, like the right qualifications. Will that do for a start? We were all so keyed up and ready to go, we'd ignored the most important things. Not one of us is anything like a business woman, and that's only part of the trouble."

"Well, hang on," I spoke gently. "That's very often the way when people are trying to do something for the first time. Take Alan Sugar, for example."

"What's he got to do with it?" She didn't know whether to laugh or cry for a moment. Tears starting to roll down cheeks that were barely lifted into a half a smile – she looked perfectly beautiful.

"Listen," I said, nuzzling her wet face. "Even he had to start somewhere.

"So, listen. Have you been talking to anyone or just kicking it around amongst yourselves? You can't be expected to do it all by yourselves. There'll be people out there who can help."

"Like who?"

"Does any of you go to church?"

"You want us to pray?" Her eyes were suddenly glittering. Potentially dangerous.

"No. I think I'd be the last one to tell you that. But it could certainly be a good time to introduce yourselves to the vicar's wife. Get her to invite two or three of you around for tea. Nobody knows more local people than vicar's wives.

"Tell her what it is you're trying to do. You might be really surprised. And make sure you take Helva along. With that accent of hers, she could charm the devil himself down off a steeple! Come on, dry your eyes. They look very beautiful with tears in the corners. But you'll have me in tears in a moment."

She dried her eyes and kissed me. "Do you think it might work?"

"Only one way to find out...Shall I make us a cup of tea, or would you like a glass of wine?"

"Tea. Please." Two distinct single-word sentences. This was Mel coming back from wherever the previous desperation had taken her. "We can have some wine with dinner."

"Who said anything about dinner?" She knew I was joking.

"Oh." I knew she was joking now as well.

"Haven't you ever heard of microwaves?"

She nodded. Pouting.

I skedaddled to the kitchen to get her the tea. And talk nicely to the microwave.

Then I put my head back round the door. "Why don't you give Helva a quick call and ask her if she feels like popping round for an hour after dinner? Just so we can talk."

Sweet-talked by its lord and master, the microwave duly produced chicken in white wine sauce, the finest that Sainsburys could sell, and we coaxed it down with a couple of glasses of white Rhone left over from the night before. Yes, sometimes there were a couple of glasses left over.

"Helva said I just beat her to it," Mel said. "She wanted to pop down anyway."

# CHAPTER 26

Either great minds work alike or Helva and Mel were telepathic. Whichever it was didn't matter. What was important was they were tuned in together. And when that tuning-in took place, a major force field was created against which there was no withstanding. I wasn't sure whether to admire them, mutter a prayer or be frightened to death.

Helva had pre-empted pretty well everything Mel and I had been discussing.

She had been talking on the phone, she said, to Mrs Willowbee. Who was Mrs Willowbee? Helva was about to tell us.

"A very nice lady, and not just nice but also very helpful."

From Mrs Willowbee, Helva had discovered that there had been a mothers' and toddlers' group – she hadn't called it a commune, and neither had Helva – which had closed down due to disagreements among the mothers over who was doing all the work.

"It seemed to me it had all been very silly, what you call a tempest in a tea-cup, I think."

"Storm," I corrected. "Storm in a tea-cup. Tempest is a play by William Shakespeare, in which one of our friends, a well-known actress, was appearing recently, possibly still is."

"So," said Helva, "a tempest – storm – in a tea-cup. No one, it seems, not even Mrs Willowbee, had sat them down and talked good sense to them. So much easier to blame everyone else. No matter. The true thing is that the place where the group used to meet now does nothing. It belongs to the church, and the church would far rather it was used for..."

"The good of the community," Mel chimed in, tears forgotten, eyes bright as buttons.

"Would I be right in thinking," I interrupted, "that Mrs Willowbee is the wife of the vicar?"

"Of course," said Helva. "Did I not say so?"

"I think the two of you – you and Mel – were just too excited to think of it."

"And that's not the end of our good fortune, is it?" Mel was beaming at Helva, who was beaming back at Mel. "Mrs Willowbee was the original manager of the group and holds all the necessary qualifications or whatever they are..."

"And," Helva leapt in, "she is happy to fill in - is that what you say? - until whoever we choose can satisfy all the requirements. And the best bit – "she now grabbed Mel by both hands - "is that they won't charge us rent so long as we pay the energy bills and services and – you tell the rest, Mel – "

"No discrimination of any kind, race or religion, or disability, so long as severely affected children have their mum or equivalent there to help them if needed. Isn't that wonderful?"

By this time, Mel and Helva were performing a little hand-holding jig. Happy wasn't the word, as they say. But if it wasn't, I didn't know what was.

"Has either of you checked out the accommodation?" I just mentioned. The little jig stopped for the merest moment.

But there was time for that another day.

Both Havel and I were conscripted. While I made a cursory inspection of the plumbing and Havel sniffed in corners for anything that could be a sign of dry rot, the girls were already picturing where the Wendy House would go, and the slide and the paddling pool that would be filled not with water but with hundreds of soft, spongy balls; whether cups of tea could/couldn't be produced in the adjoining kitchen (only one way to find out, so next time bring an electric kettle), what the latest playthings were and where the money might come from to buy them.

Mrs Willowbee, who had left the four of us to explore and discuss, now put in another appearance. In the cellar beneath the church were still some toys and equipment from the original playgroup, as well as some attendance records that nobody had bothered with after the old group had fizzled out. Some of those mums had been really sorry when it closed and would surely be worth approaching.

Helva was convinced it could be done and was already talking to one of the other mums who was keen to make a start. I volunteered to prepare leaflets and write letters. For Mel there was one problem. As yet, "her baby" was only a prospect, and possibly distant at that. Until it happened, she was keen to keep working and earning.

"How about both of us going part-time?" Helva suggested. "We could then be involved in setting up and running the playgroup – and when baby time comes, we can both be full-time mothers and playgroup ladies!"

"Time to get busy," Mel told me, planting a meaningful elbow in my ribs.

"Havel also," Helva laughed. "Think of all the fun we'll have."

"It has to work," said Mel, arms now firmly around my neck.

"What has to work?" Me, being dim.

"What do you think?" said Mel.

"You, too," Helva nuzzled Havel. "No more nasty little rubber thingies."

## Interlude

Later that night.

"Can't you sleep?" (This is Bernie.)

"No. I mean no, I can't sleep."

"Excited?"

"Not sure." Not the answer I expected, but I wasn't wholly sure about that either.

"Not sure about what?"

"Everything," says Mel. "I keep thinking everything seems to be falling into place so easily; too easily. Shouldn't things like this be more of a struggle?"

"I won't say that hasn't crossed my mind." Then I take what could yet be a dangerous plunge. "You don't suppose the two of you, you and Helva, are weaving yourselves into a lovely fairy story. Because you want so much for it to be true? We humans don't always take much persuading. Suggestions start looking like promises. Promises begin to look like the finished article. But we all know you can't quench your thirst at a mirage."

"I wish you hadn't said that..."

"Why's that?"

"Because I've been lying here thinking much the same. I mean...Mrs Willowbee is a lovely person, but we know there's no such thing as a fairy godmother..."

"And Cinderella never did go to the ball..."

"I wouldn't go that far..." says Mel.

"What I'm saying, really, is we don't know much about our fairy godmother at all. I know we were overjoyed to find her. And it seems as if she was just as overjoyed to find us. But we don't really know her. We don't know she isn't a depressive, for example, taking who knows what tablets. She could be delusional."

"Hang on," says Mel, suddenly sounding fully awake. "You don't suppose the fairy godmother was on the other foot, so to speak? Maybe she had a breakdown when the other playgroup got into trouble. She might even have got into some kind of bother herself, though I don't even like to think of such a thing..."

"I love you," I tell Mel. "You're not just a pair of blue eyes, are you? There's some wonderful grey cells, too."

Mel squeezes closer. "And a great pair of tits, too, so they tell me..."

"Who's they?"

"Oh, all kinds of people."

"You don't mean both kinds of people, by any chance?"

"Could be..."

"Be serious again for a minute," I tell her. "We can't ignore this, can we? I mean, we can't press on regardless. We need to know. Otherwise we could end up being delusional as well."

Mel is getting out of bed, just for a wee I assume. I've assumed wrong.

"I'm going to ring Helva."

"What, at half past one in the morning?"

"I've got to tell Helva what we've been thinking."

"Go on, then. I wanted to do some more work on those terrific tits you were boasting about."

"When I come back, if you're still awake."

# CHAPTER 27

Mel is perched on the sofa arm, back in the living room. As Bernie would probably say, she is a sight for sore eyes, one small cotton nightie apparently not much bothered what it covers and what it doesn't. The phone is clasped between chin and shoulder while she picks at a hangnail on the other hand.

"When did you begin thinking about this?" Helva asks.

"This afternoon," says Mel. "But we didn't begin talking about it till tonight in bed. I couldn't get to sleep and I guess I was keeping Bernie awake.

"We'd both been thinking about the same thing. How easily everything seemed to be fitting in together. Do dreams really come true just like that?" She snapped finger and thumb together to emphasise her point. Bernie, who had just come into the room, had never seen her do that. Didn't even know she could. He doesn't hear, of course, what Helva is saying to Mel.

"I'm so pleased you telephoned me," says Helva. "I wasn't sure whether to telephone you. It was keeping me awake. I was thinking the same thoughts as you. But Mrs Willowbee is so very nice. Surely she cannot be a confidence trickster? She hasn't asked for money."

"Bernie thinks she may not be well," says Mel. "He thinks she may be suffering from delusions. Possibly she is taking medication that affects her grasp on things."

"That's what I think, too. Perhaps she was so upset when the older playgroup had to close, maybe she had a breakdown. Perhaps she felt she was to blame."

"What does Havel think about it?"

"Havel? I don't know. When he found I was awake, all he wanted to do was fuck!"

"Lucky you!"

"Not so. He went back to sleep again. Hey, Mel, can we meet up to talk again tomorrow? I'm missing you already. May I say something else to you? I think I love you."

Mel takes a moment to digest this declaration; not because she is shocked but because her heart misses a beat.

"Helva," she replies, "not only may you say it, you may say it as often as you like. Do you know the English word 'mutual'?"

"As in Charles Dickens's book 'Our Mutual Friend'?

"More or less. Dickens got it slightly wrong. What it means is 'both ways.' So if I tell you it's mutual, I'm telling you it's the same for me."

A little sound of pleasure escapes Helva's lips and nestles in Mel's ear. "So listen," says Mel, "shall we meet up tomorrow? How about a drink after work? Or can you manage lunch? My treat. Call me at work when you know what's best for you."

"Okay, it's a date," says Helva.

"And by the way," Mel signs off, "give it a little tickle for me when you get back to bed."

Perhaps Mel has forgotten Bernie is still in the room, though he doesn't seem to have noticed the flirtation. But then, as we know, he's been around the block himself a few times and is in no position to comment. And who knows, there might even be something in it for him.

When Mel pops back into bed, Bernie is already there. "Helva had come to the same conclusion as us," she tells him. "I'm going to get together with her sometime tomorrow, so we can have a proper chat."

"Or another improper chat," Bernie suggests, and pokes out his tongue. Which is his way of showing Mel he's not being serious. "Now, coming back to those great tits..."

"Oh, all right," she says, arranging herself for him, "but remember, we both have to work in the morning...I wonder if Helva is getting her little ladygarden tended just now..."

"You can always ask her tomorrow," Bernie tells her. "You seem to share most things."

Mel's only comment is a grunt. There will be more.

# CHAPTER 28

Mel is a bit uncertain about her lunch date with Helva, but only about where they should eat. Having made it clear the treat is on her, it can hardly be a sandwich bar; but then if she pushes the boat out (she wonders if Helva knows that expression), that might turn the friendly bite into an embarassment.

She decides on a compromise. A posh sandwich bar. When they are both sitting down, she decides to come clean about her dilemma, at which point they both dissolve into laughter. Clearly, there are sandwich joints and sandwich joints, and Mel has lit upon one that masquerades as some kind of bon viveurs' gourmet oasis. Looking around, it feels like they've been transported by some kind of blue-tooth magic into Alice's Paris.

"Can you come back in a few minutes?" Mel asks the teenage model who's taking orders. (For readers who have just spotted a glaring anachronism, this is a time-slip novel. Author.)

"I love Alice in Paris," Mel tells Helva. "It makes me feel liberated."

Helva confesses that she loves it too. "It makes me feel hungry."

"For all those lovely French delicacies?"

"Of course. The lovely French food and lovely Parisienne Alice..." It's difficult to tell whether Helva is blushing or giggling. Let's call it one-each.

"You'll have me blushing in a minute," Mel whispers. "And how will we explain that to our gorgeous young waitress?"

"Have whatever you like," says Mel, still whispering. "It's going on my company credit card."

"I think you are a naughty girl," Helva whispers back.

"I love being naughty." This is Mel in her naughty mode. "And I've hardly begun yet. You'd never believe how innocent I was when I first met Bernie."

The young girl bringing their order leans over the table from Mel's's side, and Helva catches Mel sneaking an appreciative glance at the girl's trim bottom.

"You really are naughty, aren't you?" Helva giggles again. "How did I manage to meet you?"

"Magnetism," says Mel. "You're not complaining, are you?"

(Here we have two ridiculously attractive young women, fencing with each other over crab sandwiches and safety-first, alcohol-free bubbly. Better safe than sorry. Oh, and fencing delicately with feet and ankles beneath the table. It's something more than a meeting of minds.)

"You do remember," Mel intervenes, "we were meeting to decide what to do about the playgroup project..."

"...And yes, before you try to say I haven't even thought about it, I'll tell you what I think we should do first."

"Please do, my wise one." Mel is entirely sincere, though smiling nonetheless.

"Thank you. I think we should make contact with the Reverend Willowbee and ask him, perhaps, whether the church authorities would be agreeable to our application."

"And?"

"And see what he says. Perhaps she hasn't told him. Perhaps there are good reasons why the other playgroup had to close. And if he says 'Oh, wonderful' – then wonderful. But if he says 'Oh, dear!' we should probably withdraw."

"I know one thing that is wonderful," says Mel.

"Yes?"

"You! With your looks and brains, you would make some lucky woman..."

"Stop," says Helva. "What you were about to say, stop. It must not be said. I feel the same as you. I want you as you want me. But as friends. Friends, as they say, with benefits perhaps. This would be no problem for Havel. He understands me and he loves me. Perhaps it is the same with you and Bernie?"

Mel places her hand softly over Helva's. "You are so beautiful and so honest. So let me be honest with you. I wouldn't ever leave Bernie, not even for you. But if you ask me if I am happy having you in my life, you know the answer already. You were very brave on the phone last night. And I'm so glad you were. Or we might not be here, having this conversation.

"Yes, I feel love for you. Is it the same as being in love? I'm truly not sure. But I know I love the love that we share, you and I. Now kiss me."

"Here in the restaurant?"

"Why not?" They stand. They face each other, quite close, like any two women friends just parting. Mel places her hands under the Finnish girl's elbows and leans towards her.

Their lips meet. Not passionately, but significantly.

Their lips meet. Meet and linger.

"So how did you get on with Helva?" Bernie asks that evening.

"Problems solved, or hopefully."

"What are you going to do?"

It occurs to Mel later that they hadn't actually settled who was doing what, but she'd plunged in anyway. "Helva's going to track down the Reverend. That's Mr Willowbee, of course. And then she'll test the water with him. As much as anything, it's a question of finding out how much he knows. He'll certainly know if it's some kind of one-woman show – which it perfectly well could be, of course, so long as she's not slightly doolally."

"Did you just say what I think you said?"

"Probably."

"Oh, dear! I'm ashamed of you."

"You don't look it. What about an early night?"

"With or without your girlfriend?"

"She's not my girlfriend."

"Yet."

# CHAPTER 29

As summer drifts into autumn, the Bravo household seems to have settled on a more even keel. "Frame" actually wins a small magazines' award that Bernie hadn't even known it was entered for (something to do with Brendan Madders, he suspects) and Brendan, who now controls the magazine's purse-strings, decides Bernie deserves a salary increase.

There is no further news of his errant predecessor Brian, or of Brian's mysterious Frieda-Hari, both of whom are still off the map, possibly somewhere in eastern Europe.

Meanwhile, closer to home, the talk of babies has faded from the front pages for the time being. Helva and Mel are noticeably less broody. They smile a lot more, especially at each other.

It follows that the playgroup project has ceased to be a top priority. Bernie doesn't have a great deal to say on this subject, probably because anything he does say may, he thinks, be taken the wrong way.

Havel is looking for work. He and Helva are mainly living on what she brings in – not very much, when all's said and done – which was why they'd been so keen on setting up the playgroup commune.

There comes the night, inevitably, when he drops the bombshell that Helva has been dreading. He's decided to go back on the North Sea oil rigs.

It isn't so much that the work is dangerous – which they both know it is – but that she knows how much she is going to miss him. And she doesn't want to go back to Finland. Being back with her family is not an experience she wishes to repeat.

It isn't that they are unkind, she says. Both families are almost unbearably kind, which would make going back even worse. It would feel like failure. And she loves living in London.

As she tells Mel, she would rather take a second job washing dishes than go home to mum.

The two of them are sitting together on the sofa when Bernie gets in from a film preview. Not that seeing them like this surprises Bernie in the least, they are almost like sisters, but he can see Helva has been crying.

It's something that always upsets him. He's witnessed his mother crying all too often over the years, frequently with his father towering over her, fists clenched and eyes half closed in fury.

Bernie is the eternal knight in shining armour, no maiden in distress is ever left – well, in distress. He's the kind of man who's never without a kind word or a clean tissue. Nor is he now. He kisses Mel, as is his customary homecoming greeting, then plops down on the sofa on the other side of Helva, who now finds herself surrounded by love radiating from both directions.

"Spill," he tells Helva, who understandably looks puzzled.

"Spill? Spill what?" Helva frowns. "You want me to move?"

"No, no, stay just where you are," he tells her, fanning out both hands in a calming gesture, as though trying to settle a young horse. "I mean, spill the beans."

"It means tell Bernie what you've just been telling me," says Mel.

"Okay, so nothing to do with beans or peas?" repeats Helva. "It's Havel. He thinks he must go back on the oil rigs to earn some money, or we cannot afford to live..."

Mel wraps a comforting arm around Helva's shoulders and squeezes. It's a good squeeze. Bernie can always tell a good squeeze, even when he isn't the one on the receiving end.

Meanwhile, Helva spills the beans. "London is so costly," she concludes.

"She doesn't want to go home to mum," Mel adds.

Bernie nods, understanding that perfectly well. "But surely that isn't the only answer?" he suggests.

"I was thinking..." Mel begins.

"Let me guess."

"We could make room for Helva here. Especially if we were able to rearrange the ironing room and put a settee or divan in there..."

"For me, I suppose," says Bernie.

"No. For the King of England," Mel gently rebukes him. "For Helva, of course."

She turns to Helva. "At least, it would give you time to see how things work out for Havel. I don't think they really approve of girls on oil rigs anyway...It's supposed to be unlucky or something."

It takes a moment for Helva to realize Mel isn't joking. "At least give it some thought," Mel tells her. "You're practically part of the family. And it would be fun anyway."

It would be more than fun, of course; it would be a different way of life. But they get on well enough, anyway. And Mel wouldn't mind. As for Bernie, well, his father had always said he'd grow up to be "a hippy or something", which was one of the old man's milder accusations. "Anarchist" was more typical – well, he didn't mind that. For anyone who knew their Orwell, it was a badge of honour. So why disappoint the old reprobate?

"Do you want to give it a go then?" he asks the two women. "If Havel is serious about the oil rigs, that is. First things first, though. Who's hungry?"

Rather than start cooking, Bernie legs it to the chippie, leaving the girls to carry on talking.

## Interlude

Welcome to my mind.

All creative people, writers especially, are damaged goods somewhere along the line. They feel the need to explain themselves, and at some point they begin spinning lies: some are little white lies, some damned great whoppers.

This book is a sequel, of course, a follow-on from "Little Boy Bruised", which tells the blow-by-blow story of a child's – and then a young man's – life as a victim of terrifying abuse, to which his mind's only response is years of psychological damage; damage which will lead to childhood PTSD and borderline personality disorder and multiple personality problems. (Not exactly a psychotherapist's description, perhaps, but a victim's first-hand experience, making up in colour what it lacks in good clinical theory.)

Principally as the result of my father's constant, fortunately unsuccessful, attempts to beat out my infant brains (sorry, but that's what it was), I've been two different people for most of my life.

It took me a long time to realise this.

When I was a child, there was the Good Bernie, a talented and studious little kid who loved reading and writing, enjoyed school, made loads of friends and won prizes for his work.

As time went by, however, Bad Bernie began to make his presence felt. I began to feel inexplicable urges to misbehave in various antisocial ways from the moment I was left alone to experiment. Curiously, my mum's best friend Tony – a lesbian friend – seemed to sense that I was two people: Bernie, when I was good, she used to say, Barnie when I was bad.

Evenings, if alone, I would run around our quite small town-garden stark naked. Just for the excitement of breaking a rule. It excited me.

Taking my clothes off became an obsession and, in my nudity, I would climb up on the roof of the adjoining tennis club and peer through a crack in the glazed roof of the shower room to watch the players showering and, sometimes, the frolicking. It was exciting, not least because of the risk I would be spotted.

I would stand in front of my parents' bedroom mirror when the house was empty, bending over to study my own bum and the little forbidden hole in the middle. Someone had evidently been taking liberties down there – I don't know who – because I looked for items I could poke into the hole, which again excited me.

The older Bad Bernie wouldn't go to school if he didn't feel like it – and would then forge letters to explain his absence, signing them with his father's name. (A death wish, do you suppose?)

Bad Bernie vandalised the scout hut, again while he should have been at school. He left an obscene note for the cub mistress to read and he made indecent calls to the lady operators at the telephone exchange. He stole sexy knickers off neighbour's washing lines. And nobody knew it was going on. This itself was another Bad Bernie thrill.

Good Bernie never did any of these things. But from the moment he knew there was no one to watch him, he would feel a powerful change come over him. Bad Bernie had taken over.

I would be aware of the duality all through my adolescence. I can sometimes feel it even now, but now I understand and can control it. Probably I'm just less interested.

But this duality would lead to far more serious consequences during my teens – see "Little Boy Bruised", also on Kindle – and change my life dramatically until my loving, caring wife helped me change it back again.

I think that writers, many of us, anyway, write because we feel a need to mend things, to put things right. We want to create substitute worlds where things happen differently. Thriller writers may want to be heroes. Writers of romances desire worlds where they are charmed, seduced and maybe ravished!

Don't decry a little wishful thinking. Writers need it – and not just writers. Without it, life – even in books – would be so much less enthralling, exciting, romantic, frightening.

Don't push too hard for documentary truth. Lie back and enjoy the ride.

# CHAPTER 30

When Bernie gets back from the chippie, there's a brightness in the apartment that wasn't there before. What is it? It's hope. Hope that life may stop playing silly buggers, allow them to take charge of their own lives, and live the way they want.

A little brightness, a dash of hope, a bright tablecloth, real cod and chips, a bottle of halfway decent plonk and – take it from Bernie – the world can look (and smell) a better place. Nothing feels right on an empty belly.

Add a few smiles straight from the heart and it can almost feel like Christmas.

"Have you girls been talking?" Bernie wants to know. "Have you had the chance to talk to Havel?"

"Yes to all that," says Mel. "Let's plate up the food and we can talk while we eat..."

It was right, what Mel had been saying before Bernie went out. They were like a family. Mel and Helva could practically be sisters. It would be a crying shame to break up what they'd found. Okay, so it was an unconventional arrangement, but couldn't that be said about their whole way of life? Queen Victoria was long dead, people lived the way it suited them. He suddenly remembered Janis

Joplin's famous remark, "If it feels good, do it!" Janis been talking about something else again, of course.

Let's not go there.

But could their unorthodox, extended family endanger the relationship between Mel and himself? There was a question, if you liked.

Bernie didn't think so. Having Helva with them didn't amount to an "either or" situation, it was an "as-well-as" situation, one more ingredient that added extra colour, extra flavour, to all their lives.

He didn't lust after Helva, he told himself, pretty as she was. He simply took pleasure – a gentle pleasure – in the way the two young women found enjoyment in each other. It was innocent, like watching kittens preen each other.

He wasn't tempted, he found, to creep around spying or eavesdropping on them. That rather surprised him. In a curious way, he wasn't curious.

Perhaps he was less than the complete man after all.

But whatever it was they had – and he wasn't so naive he didn't know – it was something precious to both of them and he felt no more tempted to partake than driven to intervene. He just found their joy infectious. Perhaps it was a reflection of the love he'd been deprived of as a child when his father came home from the war. That deprivation which had led him to explore so many different and dubious paths as an unloved teenage boy.

He no longer felt unloved. He and Mel loved each other. They both loved Helva. And Helva simply radiated love all around. It truly did feel like a family, and Bernie loved that too.

Whether the family circle would stretch to accommodate Havel when he came back from the oilfields was another issue. That was for Havel and Helva to consider.

But he was hopeful, and hope had taken him a long way in his still fairly short life.

He felt he was a lucky man. The way ahead looked encouraging. And Mel had started getting broody again. Life was full of love and possibility.

# CHAPTER 31

Bernie is playing with words. Isn't that what writers do? Ever since he left school, every penny he has ever earned has come from writing. Many different kinds of writing, to be sure, but every one of them starting with a blank sheet or screen, which can only be filled from the grey cells inside his prematurely greying head.

Some would say he's set himself a pointless task on this occasion. Something inside tells him that the little grouping that now constitutes their happy household should have a noun of its own – or at least a noun that sums it up. (What kind of a mind would struggle with something so absurd? Answer: Bernie's mind.)

Family is out for a start. Sounds too close to Manson. Commune sounds too formal and rule-bound. Community? What, of three – or will it be four? This, he decides, isn't leading anywhere. So he abandons logic and switches his search from the mind to the heart, something he learned in the advertising business. And as so often before, the little light bulb comes on inside his head.

"Kibbutz!" How wonderful is that? Just a little kibbutz of their own, everything shared including the household tasks, income, worries (hopefully not too many of them), everything that makes it work – shared among them.

Okay, he tells himself, so it's a bit small to be a real kibbutz, and there's nowhere for them to be growing oranges, but the idea, the spirit, is too beautiful to be thrown out.

Now all he has to do is sell it to the others. No; first he has to persuade them of the need for a name. They'll probably start by laughing – or frowning – he's not sure which would be worse. But he thinks he can do that. (Aren't writers salesmen underneath it all?)

At which point he'll suggest "kibbutz".

A voice tells him it probably needs what the admen call a creative rationale. But if it gets to that point, he decides, he'll have to wing it. He's done that before, too.

He's been doing all this creative thinking on the way home from the office. Both girls are already home, in the kitchen, chatting and sharing a bottle of cheap Bulgarian red.

"Save some for me," he says.

"Of course," they tell him, and he gets a kiss from both of them.

It's a ping-meal night, as it has to be when they've all been working. But it makes for a relaxed atmosphere. Eat with a fork, talk with your mouth full, wash down with honest plonk that doesn't break the bank. Who could ask for more, apart from the clever dicks on TV always telling you how you should eat?

"Helva has some news," says Mel.

Bernie looks at that young woman with an encouraging smile.

"It's Havel," she says. "I have a text from him. He will not come back to England, he says."

"Did you expect that?"

"I don't know what I expect. He comes back, he doesn't come back. I get tired of asking him."

"And where does that leave you?"

Helva frowns for a moment. Then her face clears. "Here," she says brightly. "It leaves me here."

It's Mel's turn. "Here, of course – where else would it leave her?"

"Sorry," Bernie says, shaking his head at his own stupidity. "What I meant, Helva, was – How do you feel about it, and does he want you to go with him?"

"As if I care what he wants," she answers. "Does he care about me? He can go to hell as far as I'm concern!"

"Good for you," says Mel. It's no time to be correcting her English.

"And you'll tell him so?" says Bernie.

"I tell him so already. I tell him he can go to hell."

Mel claps her on the shoulder. Bernie can't stop himself laughing. Which sets Helva off.

Mel is first to recover. "I think we all need another glass. Have we got another bottle?"

Bernie disappears for a moment and returns with a bottle of Oz red that ought to be breathed, but why worry? There are more important things in life.

He tops up their three empty glasses, splashing a bit, but nobody's paying attention.

"To us," he toasts, as he raises his glass.

"To us, to all three of us," says Mel.

"To all of us," adds Helva, with a smile as wide as a spiv's kipper tie.

"If you're happy," Bernie tells Helva, "we're happy too. I'm so pleased, I can't tell you."

"You can tell me," Helva says. "Please tell me."

Bernie gets up, places his hands on her shoulders and a noisy kiss on her lips. "Now," he says, when he pulls back, "did that show you how pleased I am?"

"For god's sake, don't encourage him," says Mel, giving her a girl-hug.

When they settle down again, Bernie looks serious for a moment. "Helva," he says, "I'm sorry to bring this up, but are we going to have any problems with your papers?"

"No," she says, shaking her head and smiling at him. "No problems. I grew up in Finland, but I was born here in England. I am a British subject. I have birth certificate and now I have passport too. So no one is coming bang-bang on the door in the night.

"So, mister," she adds, "you don't get rid of me that easy. Here I stay...and make love to your wife!"

She bursts out laughing, coils her arms around Mel's neck and kisses her firmly. Far from resisting, Mel kisses her back.

"We're going to have to get a bigger flat," says Bernie.

"We're going to have to get a bigger bed," says Mel. Bernie knows she isn't joking. He raises his glass in a toast. "Welcome," he says, "Welcome to the kibbutz!"

"Kibbutz?" says Helva. "That's Jewish, isn't it? Like a farm where everybody shares and works together? I think that's lovely."

"Bernie's idea," says Mel. "You're right. It is Jewish."

"Is Bernie Jewish?"

"You wanna see my membership?" says Bernie. "Or will you take Mel's word for it?"

They collapse again into a giggling girl-hug.

"Suit yourselves, won't you?"

# CHAPTER 32

According to my father, I was an anarchist – at that stage, merely a rebellious teenager – but I guess, as the years went by, I took an undoubted pleasure in proving him right. If he wanted an anarchist in the family, I'd oblige him. In my own way, of course.

I had become editor of an award-winning and tolerably intellectual magazine which, let it be admitted, clung to life by the staples in its spine and the good grace of its chairman. I had met and married a beautiful young woman, blue-eyed and gold-curled, who would one day – well, actually two separate days of two separate years – bear me two gifted sons, and I would enjoy a life as unconventional and happy as his own had been peculiar and cruel.

What's more, as a couple, Mel and I had made room in the family for another young woman we both loved and who loved both of us. We grew, as a family, organically – in number, in mutual affection and collective support.

And if we knew, as everyone must, that it couldn't last for ever, we were no worse off than anyone else, and far happier in the meantime. If anyone thought we were immoral, they either got over it or got over us. We didn't much mind which. Mostly they envied us.

Would my father have regarded it as anarchy? Very likely and, if so, I was more than happy to think so.

By comparison, my father was a foul-tempered wife-beater and child-beater, who would die unloved, unmissed and alone except for his anarchist son whose sole reason for being at his hospital bedside was to be sure that he hadn't by some means eluded the grim reaper.

By sheer good luck, or thanks to resilient genes, I had survived the horrors he inflicted on me. So had my tough old mum. We were beaten, battered (yes, there is a difference) and terrified by the monster she had somehow contrived, or been persuaded, to marry. He could so easily have become a murderer.

His savagery and its inevitable results are described in "Little Boy Bruised", also on Kindle.

The real problem, of course, is not the visible bruises, which fade, but the damage which becomes visible only on a brain scan: the rewiring of the brain itself and the resulting impairment of functions so vital to everyday life. Even more damaging, however, is for a child to witness such attacks on its mother.

What I describe in "Little Boy Bruised" is what happened to me and to her: a blow-by-blow account, literally, of a frightening and miserable time.

It left me with Childhood PTSD and Borderline Personality Disorder, both debilitating mental conditions that can leave the victim dependent on medication and struggling to cope with normal day to day interactions, for the rest of his or her life.

In my case, the villain of the piece got clean away with it. Or thought he did.

But survival is an instinct. And perhaps there is a place called hell.

# EPILOGUE...

At the time of writing, the little kibbutz is thriving. Mel is blossoming, happily pregnant, and Helva – rather than being envious – is happy for Mel. One baby at a time, they seem to have decided, and I'll drink to that. Unless, of course... but twins don't run in our two families.

Meanwhile, time has healed one or two rifts.

Helva and Havel are friends again but have no intention of getting back together. Helva likes it far too much in London and Havel just isn't a big city boy.

Mum writes little letters from time to time and I write back. She seems well, which is good. The old devil, my father, has quietened down a good deal. He's now got what mum calls a dickey ticker – serves him bloody well right – so he tries not to excite himself (excite himself!) like he used to, presumably because he doesn't like the idea of dropping dead.

Mum loves the way the three of us now live together – and to think I was worried about telling her – and she can't wait for Mel to have the baby. One way or another, we'll invite her up.

Then a notelet turns up from Berenice of all people.

"Darlings," she typically begins. "You'll never guess what – I'm doing Brecht and enjoying it immensely!! It gives me the chance to give vent to all my pent-up passions, which you should know all about, Bernie. You always were my ideal male lead – such a pity you never took up acting! Still, if you ever change your mind... The rumour mill says Mel's having a baby! Yours I hope (only joking). Give her my very best love. I'd really love to be a godmother, by the way, but I don't suppose you do godmothers, do you?"

"Tell her we live in a kibbutz!" says Mel. "That ought to give her something to think about!"

Then two letters turn up in the same week. I'll let the first one speak for itself.

"Bernie, hi!

"First things first. Congratulations on the award you picked up for 'Frame'. I always told you you'd make a better job of it than me. I'll have to see if I can pick up a recent copy. They used to have it in the Kremlin library, you may remember, that is until you picked a fight with the Ministry of Culture.

"You've probably heard all kinds of rumours about me, mostly true I expect. Well, I'm in Switzerland at the moment – good old neutral Switzerland – and I'm living with Frieda. No doubt Brendan Madders has filled you in about her. She's very nice actually, a socialist of course, so we suit each other very well.

I haven't included a return postal address. Wish I could but it wouldn't be a very good idea. Carry on the good work with 'Frame', and if by any chance you're at the Festival of Short Film in Vienna next year, you might keep an eye open for a shady figure in a doorway or wherever...

Best regards, Brian

PS - Please don't show this to anyone else. And if you want to keep it for sentimental reasons (!), do make sure it's somewhere well out of sight. B."

I show it to Mel, of course. "Could we do Vienna, do you suppose?" she asks.

Maybe we could.

I've made my alter ego, Bernie, keep the following letter for last. The predictable obsession of a tidy mind, you might suppose, but that would be to pre-suppose Bernie and I share such a thing in the first place. Pardon my smile.

The letter comes from an address in the Cotswolds. It's rather beautifully typed (by a secretary or amanuensis, perhaps) on marbled paper and has come from one Group Captain ********, Royal Air Force Rtd.

My first thought is to have Mel read it to me.... My nerveless fingers don't seem to want to grasp the posh letterhead.

The feeling, or rather lack of feeling, reminds me of that afternoon when, as a child, these selfsame fingers wouldn't or couldn't do up the buttons on my small boy's trousers after I'd been for a pee and I'd had to persuade a somewhat dubious pal to help.

My pregnant Mel is having an afternoon nap, however, so I steel myself and start to read.


"Dear Mr Bravo,

I understand from a mutual friend that you have been endeavouring to uncover any information at all concerning your father's RAF service during World War II.

As you yourself discovered, he seems to have disappeared off the map so to speak, and off official records. How the latter occurred is anybody's guess, but is probably due to sheer carelessness on the part of a records clerk somewhere, rather than anything more sinister.

What I can tell you, and the reason I am writing to you now, is that I was actually his Commanding Officer in Egypt for most of 1942-43. I write in confidence, as you will appreciate.

Your father was a good-looking and smart young airman. If only that had been the whole story. He had, however, an unfortunate character defect that outweighed any initial favourable impression. He could not stay out of trouble. I almost lost count of the number of times he was marched into my office by the Flight Sergeant on some charge or other relating to disciplinary matters. He had a short fuse, lost his temper only too easily and fights frequently ensued.

The fights were not always his fault, but it just doesn't do to have a very thin skin when you are one of a group of young men who live with stress, danger and, a lot of the time, boredom. The infractions had, of course, to be dealt with. We were, after all, there in the desert to fight Germans not each other.

He had one thing, however, that outweighed all this. He was a damned good wireless and radio telegraphy specialist and, quite frankly, we would have been lost without him on numerous occasions. Otherwise, I might well have been tempted to get him transferred out of the unit.

Fate took a hand as it happened. He contracted typhoid fever, from which he very nearly died. The cause was traced to a dead rat which was discovered in a large tea-urn that ground crew were allowed to help themselves from when coming off duty.

I should not perhaps tell you this, but it was rumoured the dead rat was a farewell "gift" from another airman who had scores to settle with him. We didn't have time for a major investigation.

I hope this note answers at least some of your questions. No need to thank me.

Yours sincerely
Etc., etc.


I wasn't sure whether to laugh or cry. It did seem as though I owed Brendan Madders an apology for doubting his version of events as told to me over the boozy lunch at his club.

And should I tell him I'd heard from Brian?

Should Mel and I risk getting together again with Berenice? It would be rocking the boat – and Mel wouldn't thank me. I would dearly love to see Berenice in Brecht, though...

But perhaps we could manage Vienna. Da-di-da-di-da... di da...


(END)